D0562589

MEASURING UP

BY

Nyrae Dawn

I fall into my car, letting myself sink into the brown, leather seats. What am I supposed to do now? Risk the Hillcrest Gym Rats, or my virtue in the strip club/possible gym in Ghettoville? My head falls forward against the steering wheel. Ugh, I hate it when I think stuff like that. What makes me any better than the people in Let's Get Physical? Let's face it. I know I'm not, which is why I'm sitting here pretending to be afraid of a fictional sex ring rather than getting my big butt out of this car and going inside to work out said butt.

Okay. Must get out of the car.

A car creeps by me on the left. The guy in the passenger seat smiles. It's funny; guys seem to check me out when they can only see from the neck up. I turn away, fighting the urge to yell, "Keep going, buddy!" It's what he'd do if he saw me standing up.

For the third time—yes, I said third—I get out of my car and head back to the building with the flashing neon green letters. They really need a new sign. It would help with the confusion on whether or not people are coming in to work on their bodies or dance on a pole.

I drop my head back to gaze at the sky. *Stop getting sidetracked and get inside. I want to do this. Just think of the look on everyone's face when there's a new me.* Oh, wow. That cloud kind of looks like a butterfly.

What is wrong with me? Why can't I go inside? *"Ergh!"* I stomp my feet.

"You okay?"

I stand here with my hands over my face, afraid to see who spoke. It was definitely a guy, but why wouldn't it be? That's the way it goes with something like embarrassment, right? It's either a hot guy or a gorgeous girl who reminds me of everything I'm not.

Before I seem like an even bigger nutcase, I slide my hands down to look at him. Standing in front of me is the embodiment of everything that has brought me to this place. Well, not the overweight part, but the gym part. And he's not my mom either, but he's everything else that brought me here.

My age, check.

Gorgeous, check. Sandy blond hair, a little on the longish side, kind of shaggy and in his eyes, dark, melted chocolate eyes. Mmm, chocolate. *Stop!*

Thin and muscular, with plumpish lips, check, check, and check.

—

6

His eyes hold mine and I can't help but wonder what he's thinking. *What's this girl doing at the gym? She definitely needs it. Think again, because it's not going to work? I wonder how many times she's been on a diet?*

"I hear ya," Mr. Gym Boy says, shifting a paper cup from one hand to another. "The gym seems to have that effect on people. You should go in, though. Who knows, you might enjoy it."

It's ridiculous when people say things like that. He hears me? Yeah, right. I have major doubts he knows what it's like to be me. "No, I'm not going in. I forgot I have something to do."

For the fourth time this morning I start back to my car. This was a stupid idea. What? Did I think I could come here, drop the weight I've fought all my life, and prove to the jerks at my school they're wrong about me? That Mom will finally have something in common with me? Never going to happen.

"It's okay to be nervous, ya know? I mean, if you're scared, I get it. Tons of people are scared of stuff like this."

My feet become too heavy to move. I will them to keep going, but they fight me. It's one thing to be afraid. Because I am. I'm scared as hell of a lot of stuff, but it's an entirely different thing for people to know I'm afraid. They already have enough ammo to use against me, so why give them more?

Slowly, I turn to face Gym Boy. "I'm not scared. In fact, I have an appointment with a trainer. Like I said, I forgot I had…another appointment."

His body language screams that he doesn't believe me. I think he's fighting a smile. That just annoys me more.

"Okay, if you say so."

What? *What?* Who does this guy think he is? My annoying feet march me right back over to him. Inside, I'm quaking, but I keep my face steady so he won't know. "If I say so? What does that even mean? Why would I lie about an appointment?"

Gym Boy shrugs. It's strange because even though you can tell he's one of the pretty people, there's something a little harder about him. Like he's a bad boy in disguise. Actually, I'm leaning toward wannabe bad boy.

"I didn't say you lied about the appointment. I'm talkin' more about the not scared part."

—

8

"You have some nerve. You don't even *know* me. Jerk," I mumble, but his eyes aren't on me anymore. Gym Boy slips around me and heads to the curb. Yes, I know I should just walk in and forget him, but I can't. He called me scared. Never mind that I am, but what kind of person calls you on it?

And weren't we talking? Who just walks away like that? I turn and see Gym Boy standing at a large van. The side door is open and there's a young boy sitting in front of him.

"The ramp isn't fixed?" Gym Boy asks a woman, who gets out, a cast on her arm. They all kind of look alike. I can't help but wonder if they're family.

"No. Joe got him in. Maybe one of the guys can help you get the chair out." The woman looks frazzled, in a hurry.

"Um, hello? I hate it when you guys talk about me like I'm not here." The boy pouts.

"No," Gym Boy snaps at the woman. "I can do it."

"I'm crippled, not helpless," the boy says at the same time.

"Let me help you get the chair. You can lift him and put him in." The woman starts to walk toward the back of the van.

Gym Boy walks away from the kid. "I got it. Don't want you to hurt your arm."

—

My feet propel me forward. Yes, he was being a jerk a few minutes ago, but I can't leave him to do this by himself. "I can help."

He takes me in, cocking his head a little like he's confused or shocked by my offer. "Don't worry about it. I got it."

Oh, what a shock. A boy who doesn't like to accept help. Color me surprised.

"Don't be such a boy, Tegan." The woman mirrors my thought.

I really want to say something sarcastic, but bite my tongue. Know-it-all or not, he needs help here and it would be wrong not to give it. Plus, the boy and lady shouldn't have to suffer because he's inconsiderate. "It's okay." I shrug. "You know, since I'm scared to go inside and all."

His eyes study me again, like he's trying to figure something out. Then he shakes his head, but I could swear I see the ends of his lips curl up slightly. I guess sarcasm scored me points.

The woman leads me to the back of the van. Tegan steps up beside me, still dissecting me. Not in the good way a guy can dissect a girl, but as though I'm a puzzle or experiment.

I've never seen eyes as dark as his, which is *not* what I should be noticing.

"It's one of the motorized ones so he doesn't have to wheel himself if he's tired. It's pretty heavy. When I say three we'll lift and pull it out. Just set it right on the ground and I can take care of the rest." Tegan is already leaning into the van to grab it.

I shake out of the little trance his eyes held me in and grab onto the wheelchair.

"One, two, three."

I lift and holy crap was he right. This chair is heavy. I stumble a little and then we get it on the ground. Luckily there's a ramp on the sidewalk that Tegan gets up easily before walking over to the boy.

"Do you need help with him, too?" I ask.

Tegan ruffles his hair. "Nah. This twerp is light." When he turns to me, his voice isn't playful like it was with "the twerp." "Thanks, though." A second later his back is to me. I'm obviously being dismissed.

"Wow, Teag. You really have a way with the ladies. I'm only thirteen and I'm better than you. When we get home, I'll teach you, Flirting 101." The boy laughs.

I almost choke on my tongue. Tegan flirting with me? Yeah right. Mom always tells me how beautiful I *could* be. Not am, of course, because being fat ruins everything. My bright blue eyes don't matter, my smile, my long lashes that everyone always comments on. So no, I'm sure he's blinded by my weight just like everyone else is.

I turn to walk inside. Not because he pretty much dismissed me, but because I want this.

The fact is, whoever said, "Size fourteen isn't fat" has never been in high school. At least not my private, Hillcrest school that's filled with fake boobs and laxatives. Where being perfect is a prerequisite unless you're rich enough to get in on your own, even if you're a little on the curvy side like me or have a big birthmark on your face like my best friend, Emily.

Will they believe their eyes when they see me again? Or maybe it won't even be at school. Maybe Mom will show me off at some function I have no interest in going to except to see the looks on everyone's faces. I like that thought, but only because it means I'll finally be what she wants.

"Can I help you?" the supermodel behind the front desk asks. An old computer sits in front of her.

But that doesn't matter. Behind her is the part that worries me.

The gym equipment.

All sorts of machines I don't know the names of even though I've tried them all before. Don't people realize these things are torture devises to make girls like me look bad? When I fumble to use it. When my stomach contracts on the abdominal machine. The mirrors on the freakin' wall. Who thought of that? Do guys design every gym?

My eyes find supermodel's again. She looks at me with a kind smile as I approach. Is it real or is she secretly laughing at me? I can't tell. "Um, yeah. My name is Annabel Conway. I have an appointment with a trainer in"—I look at my watch. Great. "Five minutes ago."

"Oh, cool." She pulls out a file. "It's awesome that we can get all the info over the phone now. Your mom was very nice when she called. I just need your signature on a few papers and a first and last month's payment and we're good to go."

My mom. Yeah right. It wasn't hard to pretend to be her.

It only takes me a couple minutes to finish everything. When I do, the supermodel says, "Okay, let me just get—oh, here he is. Tegan, you have a new client."

Tegan? I didn't even realize he came in. I twist around to see him approaching us. No. This won't work. "Um, I specifically asked for a girl," I tell her, trying to keep my voice low so he doesn't hear me. It was a hard choice when I called because it's not like I really want a girl to know my body fat percentage either. They're even worse than guys, but I hoped there might be someone…a little like me?

"Sorry. No female trainers." Hello bionic hearing. Gym Boy steps up beside me.

"Why didn't they tell me on the phone?" I hope supermodel doesn't think I'm checking her out because I'm not letting my gaze veer from her, hoping we can somehow cut Mr. I-like-to-call-clients-on their's-fears out of this.

"Because we had one."

I turn to face him since he's obviously going to answer all my questions. "And you don't now? It's been less than twenty-four hours."

"Only takes thirty seconds to quit."

"Do you have an answer for everything?"

"Yep. It's called the truth."

This boy is going to drive me crazy! How am I supposed to go through with this if he's my trainer? "I never lied."

"Guilty conscious? I only said I told the truth, not that you didn't."

"Umm, Teag." Crap. I almost forgot supermodel was there.

"Listen; is there anyone else I can have?"

"Well, there's—"

"No," Gym Boy interrupts. He nods toward some chairs and for some complete freak of a reason, I follow him. Maybe it's because he's not looking at me like Jerk McJerkerson right now. We sit down. This should be interesting. "I could have handled the chair, you know."

"Umm, good for you? I'll try and remember not to be a normal, polite human being next time I see you."

At first my words seem to shock him, but then his smile threatens to appear again. "As long as we're clear on that." That quickly, his voice isn't clipped the way it was when we first started talking.

"Okay, if you'll excuse me, I'm going to find a trainer who doesn't have split personalities..."

"Wait, I know we didn't get off on the right foot, but like it or not, you need me, Annabel."

"...or who isn't a jerk." I try to stand, but he touches my leg and I hurry to sit down, hoping he'll move it before he realizes how jiggly it is. He's shaking his head, but the way he looks, makes me think it's not at me.

15

"Hear me out. Since I'm such a jerk with mental issues, it's obvious you don't like me. Working out can be kind of an embarrassing thing. Since you don't like me, you won't care what I think. It'll be easier to focus on what you're doing and it'll help you reach your goals." He settles into the seat, looking all smug like he just came up with some Ghandi-like quote.

"Yes, but aren't you supposed to actually trust your trainer as well?" There. Take that.

"Hey!" He sits up straighter. "What did I do to make you feel like you can't trust me? As I've showed you, I've got the honesty thing down pat."

I roll my eyes and make sure he sees me. "Are you even old enough to be a trainer? How do I know you know what you're doing?"

I can tell by the gleam in his chocolatey eyes that he knows he's got me. But in a way, he does have a point. There are plenty of pretty boys at my school for me to worry about, why do I need to care what this one thinks of me?

"I'm eighteen. It's June, my birthday is in August. Graduated this year, but took the course, and got certified last summer. Been doing it ever since. Though I'm really not sure why I'm trying to sell myself to you."

"Ah, so this is an undercover massage parlor." It takes a minute for me to realize I made a joke with him. "Get it? Sell yourself? Sorry. It's the sign. I'm sure the answer to your question is the money, though." *Or he thinks it would be funny to see the fat girl fail.* Ugh. Why do I always do that?

Tegan's mouth tightens so slightly I can hardly tell. "I don't need your money. You can find someone else if you want. I just need to know if we're doing this or not. Do we have a deal?"

I think about Billy Mason. About all the looks I get in the school halls. About Mom and how I want to be a daughter she's proud of. How I don't fit into her perfect world. He's kind of right about the fact that I don't care what he thinks. Does it help? I think so. Then I think about my other option, which is driving into the city or the Hillcrest Gym Rats and the choice is made. "Ugh, I guess. But do we have to start today?"

Chapter Two

165.8 STILL. UGH.

Okay, so it's only been about forty-five seconds since I agreed to this, but I'm already having second thoughts. "A scale? No one said anything about telling you what I weigh."

Tegan stands beside the scale of death, looking at me like it's no big deal. "Well, what did you expect? We have to know what you're starting at so we can keep track of your progress."

"We"—I signal back and forth between us—"don't need to know. I need to know, which I do. I can keep track just fine."

Tegan sighs. I can't tell if it's an annoyed sigh or not. "If you really want to do this, we have to do it right. I swear, I'm not going to judge you."

"Pfft." Oops, did I say that? Why yes, yes I did. "Please. People always judge me." *Is she lazy? Doesn't she care about herself?* I've heard them all.

"And what did you think of me when we first met? I'd love to know that one."

How does he continually turn this around on me? The worst part is, he's right. I hate it, too. I don't want to be like the people who look down on me. Maybe I didn't look down on him, but I decided who he was the very second I saw him. Though, I did also think he's cute. I should get points for that.

This time it's me who sighs. I cross my arms, knowing he's right, but not liking to admit it. "Who are they? The boy and the woman?" I ask, partially because I want to stall, but also because I want to know.

The corners of his eyes crinkle like he's in deep thought. Who knew it was such a difficult question?

"Who do you think?" he asks, a slight edge to his voice. Obviously this isn't something he likes to talk about.

"Your mom and brother?"

A small nod is his only reply. Tegan crosses his arms. "We're not here to talk about them, though. You ready to do this?"

The way he stands suddenly tense tells me I'm not going to get any more out of him. He's my trainer so I'm not sure why I want the answers anyway. Maybe because it sucks? I feel bad for him. I can't imagine having a brother who's paralyzed, or is it just because I really, really don't want to do this? "Do we have to?" My voice comes out more vulnerable than I'd like. Stupid insecurities.

"My middle name is Edgar."

"And mine is Marie. Nice to meet you." Did this guy take one too many protein shots? Juicing it up in the locker room or something?

Tegan laughs, some of his tenseness falling away.

"No, that's not what I meant. It's a lame name, right? My mom gave me a kickass first name and then my middle name is Edgar. It's not a family name either. It's embarrassing, so…"

"Wow…" Not sure why I say that. It's cool of him to try and offer something embarrassing in exchange for something that stresses me out. He might not have wanted to give me any information on his family, but he gave me this. It's definitely not something I expected. As cool and totally unexpected as it is, it's still not the same as getting on this scale. In fact, I'm feeling a little dizzy at the thought.

"You can do this. You're here, you came back three times and then you walked in the door. Don't give up on me now."

Did he have to mention he saw me? But he has a point. I'm here and I'm doing this. I nod and take a step forward. Tegan messes with scale until it lands on 165.9. Great, it's even worse than I thought. My eyes squeeze shut, waiting for the snicker, the wise crack, but I'm greeted with silence. Pretty soon I'm begging for something. If he'll just say it and get it over with we can move on.

"You coming, Annabel?"

I open my eyes and he's standing a good ten feet away from me. He's got his clipboard in his hand. There's no grin on his face. No mocking, just a little tilt of his head again as he starts walking. This time, I follow. Maybe this won't be as bad as I thought.

Tegan leads me to this little cubical before handing me a small machine with handles. "How tall are you?"

"Five foot two."

He punches some buttons. "Okay, I need you to grip this. It's going to tell us your percentage of body fat."

I am dead.

"Nope. I draw the line there. One look at me is all it takes to know my percentage of body fat. It's like, a lot."

Tegan groans like I'm the one being unreasonable in this situation. "What? Like you would want to just offer that information to anyone?" I look at him. "Okay, well maybe you wouldn't mind, but the average people, we mind."

"I'm not just anyone, I'm your trainer—kind of like your doctor. I need this information to do my job. I can easily look it up, but this is more accurate."

The urge to stomp my feet again strikes, but instead, I rip the fat counter thing out of his hand, and hold it. Big red numbers flash on the screen, brighter than the sign out front. "29.3? That's like, a lot, right?"

It takes him a minute to reply. "Does it matter? The facts don't change. You're here to lose and we're going to make sure that happens. Let's look at the positive and not go into it picturing this big mountain to climb. We're going to take it one step at a time."

One step at a time. Okay. Though I'm sure that's pretty easy for him to say since he looks like he just stepped out of High School Elite magazine and probably has Supermodel for a girlfriend.

"One step at a time," I confirm, trying to sound like I believe it. Luckily, we wasted most of our time together with my being late and then almost walking out on the whole getting physical thing, so by the time we're finished setting up our workout days and getting a plan together, there's no time to actually do the exercising part.

Darn.

"Alright, I'm headed to get my brother and I a smoothie. So, I'll see you tomorrow?" Tegan says as he walks me to the door.

That must mean his brother is here. I can't help but wonder why. I don't ask. Instead, I say, "Smoothie?" Like the biggest idiot on the planet.

"Yeah Berry Berry Blast. My day usually doesn't start unless I've had a Berry Berry Blast."

I can't tell if he's joking or serious. Luckily—or unluckily, I don't have to. There are two girls sitting on the chairs we vacated earlier. One of them elbows the other while we're standing there. They both take in the sight of Tegan. I'll be the first to admit he's kind of on the short side for a guy, but they obviously don't care. They're taking in the view.

"Hey, T. Don't lie to the girl, you probably have at least three a day." One of them does that annoying giggle-and-wave thing.

"What? I'm not that bad. I'm going to pretend you didn't say that. You ready for your workout today?" He smiles.

Ah, so he's nice to everyone. That explains why some of the time, he actually seemed semi-cool today.

I don't give him time to walk away from me, for them. "Yeah, tomorrow," I mumble before making my way out the door.

***

Dinner around the Conway house is nerve-wracking for me. It's the one time all three of us sit down together, in the same room, talking with each other. It doesn't happen every day because Dad's a doctor and Mom spends her days making the inside of peoples' homes look as beautiful as she wishes I was, but when time permits, it's our "family time."

If you can call it that. It's always a mix of emotions for me which triggers my need for chocolate. Nothing cures nerves like chocolate. Or ice cream.

I pull out the chair to our oversized dining room table and sit down. Like the rest of the house, Mom decorated the room. It's got a royal feel to it, done in deep reds and golds, even though we're nothing of the sort. I'm pretty sure she'd like to think she is, though. The carpet's red. It's not as bad as it sounds. I actually like the shade she picked for the floors. It's when you add in the gold crown molding, the red and gold diamonds painted on one "accent wall," and the gaudy chandelier she loses me.

But when people come over, they seem to like it so maybe it's another one of my defects.

Mom comes into the room first, long, lean, and impeccably dressed, in a slim fitting business suit. I always expect the president or maybe the pope (if we were Catholic), to magically poof into the room during one of our meals. Then I could understand the extra few minutes she spends in front of the mirror just to eat some broccoli and chicken with Dad and me.

But who knows, I guess if I was as perfect as her, I would want to look the part 24/7 too.

As Dad comes into the room, wearing a pair of slacks and a t-shirt, she clicks off her cell phone. I love how Dad does that. He's a mixture of Mom's fashion and my relaxed look. He can handle the slacks, he always says, but the second he gets home from work, he replaces his shirt with the most comfy tee he can find.

"Hey, Pumpkin." Dad leans forward and kisses the top of my head, ruffles my black bob (short hair makes your face look thinner, according to Mom), and sits down at the head of the table.

"Hey, Dad." I smile at him and he gives me a kind one in return.

"I wish you wouldn't call her that, Daniel. She's too old. A young woman shouldn't be a pumpkin," Mom says.

I know most girls my age wouldn't like being called pumpkin, but I love it. He's called me that since I can remember. It's something that's ours and no one else's.

I wonder if no young woman be a pumpkin or just not the fat ones. From what I hear, Mom's parents weren't the type to have a "pumpkin," just like she isn't. According to Dad, it's why she is the way she is. Still, why does she have to take that away from me? Because now I'm not sure I want to be a pumpkin anymore. I hate her for that.

"She'll always be my pumpkin, Paulette. No matter how old she is." Dad pats my hand, giving me a smile because he thinks he made it better. I give him a squeeze so he can keep believing it.

"I understand." Mom sits down. "She's my little girl, too. I still think she's too old to be a pumpkin." She winks at me. Does she think she's doing me a favor? That I don't realize she probably thinks I'm a big, fat pumpkin every time he uses the name? That taking it away will make me more who she wishes I was?

I'm not even sure if I can be mad at her for that.

"How was your day, Mom?" While she rambles on about color patterns and the Marsh's daughters' new dresses for the Hillcrest Summer Pageant, I put a piece of grilled chicken on my plate then reach for a scoop of potatoes.

"It's the most gorgeous shade of blue…Not so much, Annabel. It matches perfectly with Bridgette's."

I don't even know how she does that. I swear her blue eyes aren't even facing my direction, but somehow she thinks she knows exactly how many potatoes I'm scooping on my plate. And she just automatically throws that line in there between Elizabeth's dress color and her mom's.

"She has one small spoonful on her plate. Don't micromanage what she eats," Dad says. I probably only have half a portion. I don't say that because I hate when they argue about me. They're so different, but they work well together. Most of the time I'm the only part of them that doesn't fit and I don't like highlighting it.

Hence the reason I ask a question I don't really care about. "What's their talent this year? They sang last summer, right?"

"Oh! It's a cheer!" Mom rambles on and on about Bridgette and Elizabeth's cheer. What the heck is that? Who wants to see a forty-five year old woman rah-rahing, trying to reclaim her high school days? Bridgette is the queen of Botox and breast implants. Oh, and she's Mom's best friend since high school. Bridgette and Elizabeth do the pageant together every year since Elizabeth turned fourteen. Every year they've won. It's the one time I'm glad Mom's not happy with my body because the pageant thing is *so* not me. But so she doesn't lose face, she likes to pretend she'd rather plan it than participate every year.

After eating half my chicken and half my potatoes, I push the rest around on my plate, pretending I'm interested. The conversation goes from the pageant to a new account Mom landed, how happy she is it's summer time and then someone nudges my foot. "Huh?"

"Your plans for the summer? Are you and...?"

"Emily, Mom." As if she doesn't know my best friend's name.

"I know." She tries to laugh it off like it wasn't an I-know-her-name-but-I-don't-deem-her-worthy-enough-to-use-it thing. "Anyway, do you guys have big plans for the summer? It's your last one before senior year."

My tongue itches to tell her. To open my mouth and let her know my only plan for this summer is to lose weight. That I'm working with a trainer so she won't tell me how many potatoes to eat or look at me like she's sorry for me. Because that's the hardest. Having parents pity you.

That I'm dealing with I'm-too-gorgeous, Tegan. The boy who's probably pretending to care...or not care about my stupid weight when he probably pities me, too. And I hate to admit it, but so Billy Mason's eyes will pop out of his head when he sees me next year and he'll regret everything he's ever said to me.

But I won't. Dad will just tell me I'm fine the way I am, as long as I'm healthy and active. Mom will look at him like he needs to be committed, give me the "eye of skepticism," and then make *me* want to be committed when she bugs me about my progress (or lack thereof), on a daily basis.

"Not much," I lie. "Just typical summer stuff, I guess. Em's taking some summer courses at the college, so I'll be on my own a lot."

"Oh, maybe you can call Elizabeth—"

I'm not sure if it's the look of horror on my face or if Dad knows spending time with Elizabeth would be torture, but he steps in. "Paulette. She's a big girl. She can make her own friends. If she wants to call Lizzy, she will."

I love my Dad for trying, but somehow his words just made it worse. We all know I'm a big girl. It's not like any of us need the reminder.

Chapter Three

165.8 I CHECKED. TEGAN WAS WRONG.

It only takes two tries to make it into Let's Get Physical. I guess it helps that Tegan made our appointments for 8:00 AM. Who gets up that early during the summer? At least it's early enough I can go home and take a nap before I meet up with Em today.

I hadn't been lying when I told my parents she's taking some college classes. She's hoping to graduate a semester early, with me. The sooner we can get out of Hillcrest High, the better.

On my second trip to the glass doors leading to Hell, I see Tegan waiting there for me. His arms are crossed, making the sleeve of his t-shirt ride up, the lining of a tattoo peeking out from under it. He's not as muscular as I thought yesterday. Definitely toned and firm, but not overbearing. He's not like Billy and his goons. You know, those guys who lift so much they grunt and their faces turn red. The grunting does give them big muscles, but I'm not sure it's worth it. Looking at his physique, I'm pretty sure Tegan isn't a grunter.

Speaking of—why the heck am I looking at his figure? My eyes snap up. Sure enough, he's looking at me, cocky little grin in place like he's God's gift to the female eye and caught me praising the Lord. Before he can comment on it—and I know he will because that's such a good-looking guy thing to do—I hold up my hand. "It's early, I'm in sweat pants, heading into the lion's den. Don't start with me right now." I stroll past him like I'm not really freaking out inside. I hear a small chuckle before he catches up with me.

"Lion's den?"

Does he really have to ask? It's pretty self-explanatory, if you ask me. "Yep."

Tegan leads me through another set of glass doors and upstairs to a room filled with all the treadmills, ellipticals, exercise bikes, and all that.

"We're going to start with Cardio."

Oh, joy! Just what I want to hear. I love running in front of people.

"It's not so bad. It's actually my favorite part. Well, not doing it on a tread, but running, outside. There's nothing like it."

I'm still trying to figure out if I spoke out loud or if he saw the look of horror I'm probably wearing on my face. For the first time I wonder how all this is going to work, if he's going to stand around and watch while I jog and everything jiggles.

"Do you like it? Jogging, I mean? I used to do Cross Country in high school."

Cross country and weights. Holy fitness buff. Is there anything to this guy other than his workouts and apparent love of smoothies? And then I remember his brother and mom. The care he showed them and the way he looked at me when I tried to help. The tightness in his face when I asked about them. Just like the rest of us, Gym Boy has his secrets.

I shake my head, still nervous to get up there and run in front of him.

"What do you do? Anything you like?"

Is this how things usually go? I'm curious what this has to do with our workout plan. "Roller blade. I used to ride a lot. Not as much anymore."

Tegan smiles like I let him in on some deep secret. "Cool. Never done it myself. Maybe I'll have to try it sometime." He pats the treadmill. "Climb up."

Sucking in a deep breath, I climb on. This is what I'm here for. I need to get over it and do it.

"Okay, we're going to start out slow today. I want to see what you can do. Twenty minutes. A couple of them walking to warm you up, then we'll go into a jog. Deal?"

We'll? I nod my head. He pushes a few buttons on the treadmill. When the belt starts moving I do too. Tegan jumps on the one next to mine. Oh, nice. Is he trying to show me up or something? But to my surprise, he keeps it at a steady walk like I'm doing. It doesn't take a brain surgeon to know what he's doing, that he probably fears if he doesn't stay up here with me, I'll bolt. There's a part of me that wants to run because hello? This is embarrassing. On the other hand, I appreciate it because somehow, it helps not to do it alone.

Before he thinks I'm ogling him again, I face forward. We're both quiet until Tegan asks, "You ready to speed up?"

"I've been counting down the steps!" I tease.

He chuckles. "You're funny. Go up to 3.8 and see how you handle that." It's not too bad, which is nice so I fall into a jog. Tegan's right there with me, doing the same thing. The urge to talk to him bubbles up in my throat, but I don't risk it for a couple reasons. The most important one being I've been at this for a few minutes now and I'm slightly out of breath. The last thing I want is to start gasping at the boy.

So, I keep my eyes on the timer instead. I guess like a watched pot never boils, a watched clock never ticks.

———

34

"Hey, Tegan. Why are you up here?" A pretty, long-legged brunette walks up next to his treadmill. Who does that? Just stands there talking to someone while they're sweating and running? Okay, so Tegan isn't sweating like I am, but still.

"Just working out with Annabel."

Legs looks back and forth between Tegan and I, but I don't pay her much attention for fear I'll fall and eat treadmill if I do.

"Oh…so we're still on for tomorrow, right?"

It would really be cool if I had my iPod right now to help me block this out. I shouldn't want to—I don't know why I do—but I sort of want to hear what Tegan has planned with this girl. I'm imagining all kinds of sordid things when he says, "Yep. 9:30 AM, just like every Sunday."

So she's a client.

A 9:30 client.

Nice. He might go from me to her. Hopefully we don't share any of the same days.

She flips her hair over her shoulder. "Looking forward to it. I was thinking…maybe after you get off we could, like hang out or something?"

Oh, God. I really don't want to hear Tegan and Legs make plans to go out.

"Um, thanks, but I can't. I have to take my bro—I have an appointment."

"Oh." She looks at the ground and I actually feel kind of bad for her, but it doesn't last long. I'm thinking about Tegan, wondering why he changed what he was going to say.

"I'll see you later." Legs walks away.

There are times my mouth just goes and I'm unable to stop it. This is one of those times. "Pick up chicks here often?" Ugh. What is wrong with me? It's not like I care.

The treadmill starts to slow, indicating our twenty minutes is up.

Tegan jumps off. "I'm pretty sure I just told her no."

"How old is your brother? It's him you'll be with tomorrow, right?" Why won't my mouth stop moving?

Tegan groans, mumbling something that sounds like, "I knew it." Then to me, "We're not here to talk about what I do or don't do, or about my family. We're here because you wanted to make a change. If this is really what you want, I want it for you, but you're going to have to decide right now."

Now I feel like a bitch again. I'm judging him. Again. How many times have people done that to me? Not only that, but I'm being pushy about his family. It's not like I want people to ask me why my mom can hardly stand the sight of me, so I shouldn't be getting into his business. I lean against the rail of the treadmill. "You're right. I suck. I get nosey and throw huge walls of sarcasm up when I'm uncomfortable." Suddenly, I'm beyond uncomfortable. My face flames.

He kind of tugs on his hair. "Don't be. Uncomfortable, I mean. We all have some kind of demon in our lives..." His voice trails off before he picks up my water bottle from the floor. "Huge walls of sarcasm don't rank high on the list."

I'm not sure where it comes from. Maybe the sound of his voice, but I can't help but wonder what kind of demons Tegan's hiding.

***

I wake up from my nap knowing I'll be sore tomorrow. The weights we lifted were light. According to Tegan: Less weight, more repetition is best. I definitely felt the burn and dread the ache a full night of sleep will allow to set in.

Since I crashed as soon as I got home, the first thing I do is take a shower so I can head out to meet Em. Should I tell her about the gym? I know her. She's not like me. She'll give me crap for going, assuming I'm doing it for all the Billy's at school, which I guess I am. But it's not like I *need* their approval, I'm doing this to prove a point. I'm doing it for me…I think.

But there's even more to my reason for not wanting to tell her. For not telling anyone. I mean, beside the fact that I don't want people to know if I fall on my face trying. For some reason, I want to hold onto this. Something I have that's mine. Not Mom's to micro-manage, Dad's to defend, Em's to get all emo about. It's something only myself—or Tegan, I guess—can control. If no one else knows, I don't have to worry about damage control or avoid confrontations from anyone in my life.

Shower complete, I dress in a pair of black jeans, despite the heat. My legs are flabby so I always wear jeans or capris, and black is slimming, right? That's what Mom always says. After putting on my light-blue, button up, short sleeve shirt, I add a little mascara to my eyes. They're my favorite thing about myself and one of the only things I get compliments on. They're a strange color. Almost icy in their blueness. I run a brush through my hair and call it good.

———

A few minutes later I'm heading to meet Em in our spot. She doesn't like me going to her house, which I don't get. I'd love a mom like hers. Not that I don't have a good one, but Mrs. M is...loving? Em thinks it's because she knows how miserable Em's life is so she's trying to make up for it by being overly attentive. I'm a little unsure of how that's a bad thing.

The hard part is she doesn't like coming to my house either because Em is...well, I guess she's just like her mom, but she doesn't realize it. Mrs. M wants to make things better for Em, while Em's overly protective of me. The only difference is where Mrs. M is all hugs and smiles, Em is all sarcasm and, well, kind of rude comments. There have been way too many times she's wanted to let that out on Mom, but since I won't let her, it's easier if we avoid my place as much as possible.

Since neither of us are real social people, we always meet up at the park when it's nice, or if we need to stay indoors, there's this hole-in-the-wall coffee house that doesn't have name brand attached so the kids from Hillcrest don't go. The park is huge, with a skateboarding area, baseball, and all that, and this little circular area with a little pond, ducks, and a couple gazebos. Amazingly, it's never crowded. Once in a while on the weekends, we catch a party or something and have to bail, but usually it's only littered with a few people here and there. Probably other outcasts like us.

I get there early and head back to our favorite gazebo, close to the pond where we usually feed bread to the ducks.

"Hey." Em plops down beside me, wearing her signature black, another reason Mom scoffs at her. It's different than the kind of black I wear. For Em it's head to toe. She's really not Goth or anything, but it's not often you see the girl wearing any different color. Instead of just wanting to slim down, though, I think she hopes it will somehow make her disappear.

"Hey you," I say, nudging her when I notice she's keeping her head tilted down. It drives me crazy when she does that. I sort of get it with other people, but there's no reason for her to try and hide her birthmark from me. It's strange how she can be so strong yet so vulnerable at the same time. Like I said, if someone looks at me wrong, Em's quick to give it to them, but she struggles to make eye contact for herself. "Did you bring the bread?"

"Yep." She pulls half a loaf out of her bag before sliding a lock of her brown hair behind her ear. It's funny how quick she warms up when it's just me. She wouldn't do that with anyone else because it gives a prime look at the oversized, brown birthmark on half of her neck and the side of her face. It only takes me a second to block it out.

Sounds crazy, but it's true.

"How were the classes, Miss. Overachiever?" It's the most ridiculous thing I can say.

"Yeah, because I'm the overachiever out of the two of us. You can do anything, Bell, and we all know it."

I flash to the gym. For some freak of a reason, that makes me think about Tegan. About how he ran with me because I needed it.

"You're smiling. Why are you smiling?"

I grab some bread from Em and toss it at the ducks. "I'm not smiling." Was I smiling? Why would I smile thinking about the torture that is the gym and Tegan?

"Um, yeah you were."

Suddenly I feel really guilty for not telling her about the gym.

I blame it on my whole fear of failure thing. How typical is it for someone to try to shed a few pounds and fail? But the fact is, if anyone would get it, it would be her. Still, I'd have to hear about how lame it is, how I'm fine the way I am and if she ever saw Tegan, it would be over. She doesn't trust anyone, and even though I don't trust him either, my huge wall of sarcasm has nothing on hers. "I don't know why I'm smiling, Em." Which I don't, so I'm not lying.

Lucky for me, Em gives up, something she usually doesn't do easily. We hang out for a while, making sure to feed the baby ducks more often than the adults, then she pulls her laptop out of her bag and we each buy some more music for our iPods. I'm a little more careful than her because I have a big fat bill I have to pay to Tegan and if I spend too much I'll either be screwed or have to ask my parents for more. It's not a big deal, because they'll give it to me, but I'm not really the blow cash kind of girl so they might wonder what I'm spending it on.

We're out here a few hours when we decide to brave my house. If we get home before Mom, I can usually get Em out without risking a Mom vs. Emily smack down. We're packing up her stuff when I hear a familiar laugh in the distance.

"It's hot as hell and you're still wearing all black and a sweatshirt? Don't tell me you're going to be one of those kids who show up to school with a machine gun, Monroe." Billy's walking with a few other guys from our school. The other three don't say much, but they never stop him either.

"You're such a jerk," Em sneers.

Billy laughs, hitting Patrick in the arm which makes Patrick laugh, too. I guess he needs permission. "Emo chicks are funny." Billy stumbles a bit. Ah, that's what this is about. They're drunk. I've heard of them coming down this way and drinking under the bridge sometimes, but I figured it happened after dark.

"And you're a dumbass."

Billy ignores her. "What about you, cupcake? Is that your plan too? Or wait, I bet you'd take a bullet for me, wouldn't you? Love makes people do crazy things."

I actually feel my face turn red. It's a mixture of embarrassment and anger. I'm not sure which emotion is the strongest. Whichever it is, it's making me mute. Nothing I say will matter: I don't love you. I don't even like you. Well, of course I don't, but all of that's just going to make me look even more pathetic. The fat girl in denial.

"Screw off, jerk. The only person who loves you is you. Stop trying to win Annabel over. It's getting pathetic."

I want to hug and smack Em at the same time. It's amazing that she sticks up for me, but on the other hand, stop trying to win Annabel over? She just set me up to take more crap from these guys.

Billy falls to the ground laughing. This time, Patrick doesn't need a nudge to join in. Soon, all of them are laughing at my expense. Em grabs my arm and pulls me away.

"Don't go away mad! Just go away!" Billy yells during laughs. "Poor Cupcake and Birthmark. You'll never amount to anything, but don't let it get to you. At least you have each other!" His voice almost echoes as we walk farther away. I still hear it, over and over.

"They suck," she says when we're almost to our cars.

"Yeah." And so do I. I'm mad at myself for letting them get to me and mad at myself for not standing up to them.

———

44

"All boys suck. Don't ever trust them. Girls like us? They're always going to end up hurting us."

Her words shock me a little. Em's always a little of a downer, but I've never heard her talk about guys like that, like someone else has hurt her I don't know about. Right now, I don't have time to think about it. All I can think of is I know she's right. And it more than sucks.

Chapter Four

DIDN'T WEIGH TODAY. GUESS I'M NOT SUPPOSED TO DO IT DAILY. NO PROMISES.

The thought of meeting Tegan today is nauseating. It's stupid and I hate myself for it, but I can't stop running over the things Billy said in my head. Being that girl, the one who lets jerks like him make her feel like this, bites. I know I shouldn't care. Hell, I don't care, not about him, but I care about me and I don't want to set myself up to get hurt again. Not from Tegan specifically, but the whole gym thing. I feel like I'm setting myself up to fail.

I drop my head against the steering wheel, even angrier now that I feel like I am those things just because he said it. Knowing you shouldn't think a certain way and making it true are two different things. People who've never experienced it don't get it. "Don't listen to them," "There's nothing wrong with you," "Just forget about it" are just words. Sure, they may make the speaker feel better, but it's hard for the person hearing them to actually let it seep into their brains and hearts.

—

Ugh. Now I'm feeling sorry for myself and that frustrates me to no end. So instead of crying in my leather seats, I get out of the car and head inside. Like yesterday, Tegan is waiting for me, but missing is the causal smile I've seen in him. This is a painted on, total Ken doll smile. There's a slight dusting of stubble on his jaw. And his eyes, they're not as lively as the other two times I've seen him. Like he's riding the high he gets when he's giving me a hard time. Right now they look like they did when he was helping his brother out of the car. No, they look almost pained. Angry.

Strangely, I miss the other smile. Which makes no sense except that right now, I could really use some positive energy.

"Tegan, you up for an extra shift this week? Jim told me to ask you." It's a different girl behind the desk today. He turns to her.

"Do you have to ask?"

She laughs. "I'll let him know."

"Mornin'. You ready?" When he turns to me, Tegan tries to sound light. Too bad it doesn't ring true. What does he have to hide? Me, it makes sense that I have demons, but with him it doesn't.

"Not particularly. How are you?" My question-filter never rests around him. It would benefit me to remember I don't care. Not about him, Billy, or anyone else.

I'm not sure why I expect him to. He doesn't answer. Instead, Tegan signals with his head (he's always doing that) for me to follow him and I do (I'm always doing that). "Are you sore?"

Actually, I am sore, but the emotional pain from yesterday overpowers the physical. "Yeah."

"That's a good thing, ya know? We don't want to overdo it, but those are like your war wounds. It means you're working your muscles, training them." I study him for a minute, surprised at the little things I'm starting to catch. It's obvious he's upset, that for one reason or another he's having a bad day. But he doesn't talk about it. Ever. Well maybe not ever, but at least not that I've seen. Instead just focuses on my problem, which yeah, it's his job. Somehow I know it's more than that.

"You worked hard and you should be proud." His words pull me from my thoughts and switches them to another.

Poor Annabel. That's a cow name, you know. Your parents must have known you'd be fat. I've heard people who are fat as teenagers will be cows forever. Stop it! Why the hell am I letting Billy Mason get to me? "Not that it will help," I mumble and even as I do, I want to snatch the words back. Not because I don't want Tegan to hear them, but because it makes me mad at myself. Why do I let my resolve slip so easily? I believed in myself when I came up with this plan and I already doubt it, just because of dumbass Billy?

"Hey." Tegan stops me with his hand and I immediately notice how warm he is. "No doubting. The biggest thing you can do for yourself is have faith. I…you have to believe that, okay? The human body can do some amazing things."

He almost said "I" have to believe. His words fill a part of me I wouldn't have thought him capable of filling and not for the reason I would think. But the way his voice almost cracks, the depth of…well, belief in them, makes me want to believe too. Somehow, I can tell he needs it as much as I do.

"Um, okay. Yeah, I believe. Sorry. Bad day. I had to deal with this jer—never mind. Just feeling sorry for myself."

"Yeah, shitty day for me, too." Tegan stands there like he's thinking. A little smirk teases his lips and I wonder if he realizes it before I start to wonder why I noticed it. I should not be noticing things like this about Gym Boy. "Okay, I have a plan, but you have to A) not mind if we deviate from your regularly scheduled workout for a bit and B) you have to work really hard to earn it."

"What is it?" Like I'm going to agree to something without knowing what it is. Yeah right.

"I'm not telling. Let's just say we're working on that trust thing you mentioned you need to have for your trainer. I will say, it'll help and I think you'll enjoy it. I'll enjoy it too. That's all you're getting out of me, though." He crosses his arms, but this time, the tension's gone.

Is it possible for a day at the gym to screw with your head? I'm really starting to think so because before I can talk myself out of it, I find myself saying, "Fine, whatever. But this better be good."

"Deal. Let's get going then. We have a lot to cover today. I have some time between you and my next appointment, if you don't mind us running late."

That automatically makes a sheen of sweat slap itself across my forehead. Great. We haven't even worked out yet and I'm already sweating. How attractive is that? Plus, adding the words running and late together don't sound good to me at all, but I nod anyway.

Luckily it doesn't start out as bad as I thought when I find out the first item on our list is to work out a meal plan. He doesn't tell me what to eat. We just talk about what I usually do eat, he gives me a book on suggestions, a diary to write my meals in, and the amount of calories I need to stay under.

"Oh, and water. Be sure you drink a lot of water."

I nod, a little sad I'll have to say goodbye to Ben and Jerry. "What about you? You drink smoothies."

"Not you too." He groans. "Can't a guy have a sweet tooth? At least its fruit I'm reaching for and not something else."

I know he didn't mean it, but his words sting. I would be the one reaching for something else. He can have a smoothie a day because he's not trying to lose weight. He moves on, not seeming to realize how his statement affected me.

We begin our aerobic on the treadmills and to my surprise, Tegan jogs with me again. We up the speed a little and I try to ignore the easy rise and fall of his chest while I'm panting for breath. From there we head into weights and resistance training and I'm wondering when this whole idea of his is starting. So far we're basically doing the same thing as yesterday. My legs burn like they're on fire while we do some machine that is supposed to give me quads of steel. They feel more like jelly at the moment.

"Come on, Annabel. Three more. You can do this."

I push my legs up again. Yeah, I can do this. I find that, all of a sudden, I really want to. Again, I lift, pushing past the burn, focusing on the way I haven't thought about yesterday between the time we started the run until just a second ago.

"You got this. One more and then you get your surprise."

His wording makes me falter slightly, but I catch myself. Ignoring the way "surprise" sounds more like a friendly gesture than trainer/trainee one, I lift against the resistance one last time. "Oh my God." I go limp against the machine. "Is it always supposed to be tougher the second day?" I'm panting. My eyes are closed and I probably look like I had a near drowning experience in my own sweat, but right now I can't find it in myself to care.

52

"It's just because your body is adjusting and you're sore from yesterday, but you know what? You hardly flinched the whole day. You were in the zone. Not half of the resistance you had just twenty-four hours ago."

My heart finds the energy to do a happy dance in my chest. I let my head roll to the side and open my eyes. Without meaning to, I smile at him.

"You killed it today. Now you definitely deserve to kick some ass."

Huh? "I'm a lover, not a fighter. Plus, isn't it against some trainer, client code to challenge said client to a fight? Not sayin' I couldn't take you, but ya know…"

Tegan shakes his head and chuckles. "Come on, Annabel. Trust me." He holds out his hand and I let him pull me off the quads of steel AKA I-may-never-be-able-to-move-my-legs-again. As soon as I'm up, we both let go. "And just so ya know, you'd be good competition, but you couldn't take me. Not yet." He winks and walks away, leaving me no choice but to follow him. Again.

***

"Um, I'm not really much of a boxer." We're in a small room by ourselves. I swear, Let's Get Physical is like a haunted mansion on Scooby Doo. It has all sorts of secret rooms I didn't know about. There are a couple long punching bags (no clue if they have a special name) and then the little ones where you have become like Road Runner to keep up with them once they start flying.

"Are you sure you're not my girlfriend or something? I think you just like to argue with me. Where's the trust?"

"You have a girlfriend?" I blurt out and then I want to box myself for saying it. *You have a girlfriend?* Of course he does. Maybe Supermodel up front or someone equally pretty. Plus, it's not like I care.

"No, bad analogy, I guess, but you get the point. What about you?"

Why is Gym Boy asking me this? Hello. I figure sarcasm is my best defense. "Nope. Don't swing that way."

He chuckles again at me. He seems to do that a lot. "You know what I mean. But"—he leans closer to me and I catch a chill. Stupid AC—"I think you knew that. If you didn't want to answer me, all you had to do is say so." He stalls a minute and then says, "Your eyes are the craziest shade of blue I've ever seen. It's like looking in a pool or something."

I feel his breath he's so close to me. Minty and fresh. What am I doing? Or a better question is, why is he so close?

"Annabel," he whispers and I swear his voice vibrates through me. Does my name always sound like that? Almost seductive? He's standing farther away from me now, trying to get me in the mood to hit a bag, not seduce me. What was I thinking? "I want you to find that anger from this morning. I know you worked some of it off, but pull it back up and then kick its ass for good."

A beep sounds from his pocket. "Hold up a sec," he says to me before pulling out his phone and saying, "Hey."

Whoever is on the other line is talking and then Tegan replies, "Three o'clock. Again? You're going to kill yourself." More silence from Tegan. "I know I'm the same way, but that's different. It just sucks. We shouldn't have to—" He looks at me like he forgot I was in the room. The Tegan from earlier is in front of me again. The one who seems to hide behind a wall like I do. "I'll come home. I'll pick him up. No, it doesn't matter, I'll change my plans, but I gotta go."

I'm sure he doesn't give the person on the other end time to reply before he hangs up. He stands there, looking at me, breathing heavy, but obviously trying to hide it. "Ready?"

I shake my head. I know this has something to do with his brother. My heart softens a little for him. "I can help… if you need something. I mean, I know we don't know each other, but—"

Tegan cuts me off. "I don't need any handouts."

"What? I'm not trying to give you a handout. I'm trying to be nice."

"Well you don't have to. We're here for you, remember? Not me. You don't have to worry about my crap."

He gives me a tight, reassuring smile and takes a step back, motioning to the punching bag, and somehow, my body automatically starts to do what he said. Mom's hurtful remarks, every name Billy has called me and everything he's put me through. It all starts bubbling over, and despite that I've never hit anything in my life, I swing. When my gloved hand makes contact with the punching bag, it feels good. Some of that bubbling anger transfers through me and into the bag. And somehow…somehow I'm hitting for Tegan too.

"There you go, but you're not nearly as tough as I thought if that's your best hit. You're pissed, remember? This is your chance to get even."

I swing again. Tegan is behind the bag, holding it, but I didn't even see him move. My fist makes contact a third time. "That's it. Now I'm feelin' it. Let it out, Annabel Lee."

Again and again my fists make contact, harder and harder on the punching bag.

"Tell 'em how you feel. Whoever it is: parents, friends, some other jerk, boyfriend…"

"Don't have a boyfriend, but the others I do have." Not that I'm mad at Em, because she's all I have, but no matter how much I love my parents, I am mad at them. Over and over I punch. My arms are aching way more than my legs were earlier. My chest hurts I'm breathing so hard and God, I probably look like the world's biggest idiot, but I don't care.

I'm showing Billy how he makes me feel. Telling Mom how much she hurts me.

"Damn, that was a good one," Tegan says from behind the bag. "Keep it up. Get rid of it because it doesn't belong here. This is *your* time. No one else's. If they aren't motivating you, they don't belong here."

I hit harder, faster.

It's amazing how freeing this is. Like somehow I'm really showing Billy how horrible he's been to me. Showing him I don't care, even though I do.

"Whew! That one about knocked me out. Chicks who kick ass are hot."

Hot? What the hell? I know I'm not ugly. I'm not, but no one has ever called me hot before. It's too late to stop my swing. It's flying so fast and hard, I lose my target. My glove slips off the punching bag, but the momentum doesn't slow. My fist lands right in Tegan's face and he stumbles backward.

"Ouch! *Shit* that hurt."

Holy cow! I just hit Tegan. I rush toward him. "Oh my God. I'm so sorry! I don't know what happened."

He's got his hand over his left eye. "You hit me. Almost knocked me out, that's what happened."

Tegan shakes his head, like he's trying to wake himself up. When he moves his hand, I see a small bruise forming underneath it. "Man, I'm so sorry." And then I realize, I gave my trainer a black eye! Not that I like hurting people, but it's kind of invigorating just knowing I have that kind of strength in me.

"Feels good, does it? I thought you were a lover, not a fighter? Could have fooled me." I almost apologize again, but he's smiling.

"How can you smile after I gave you a black eye?"

"You gave me a black eye?" he asks.

"A little one."

He nods. "Bad ass..."

—

It's then I remember why I accidentally hit him in the first place. All the anger I just punched away comes flooding back at me. The memories. The lies. They sing in my blood, pulsing right beneath the surface of my skin. Does he think I'm going to fall for that? That I don't know he's playing me? Let's tease the poor little fat girl and make her think she's something special. I rip the gloves off and throw them to the ground. "Whatever. I'm done." Without another word, I turn and walk out, tears stinging my eyes.

When I hear his footsteps behind me, I run. As I peel away from the lot, he stands on the street, watching me go.

Chapter Five

BEN AND JERRY, I MISSED YOU

The next day isn't a gym day for me. I spend it at home and with Em. She can tell something's wrong with me, but every time she asks, I blow it off like it's nothing. It *should* be nothing, but for some reason, it's not. I feel like scum right now. Actually, worse than scum.

"Is this about that jerk, Billy?" she'd asked

I'd been honest when I told her no. Because it isn't about Billy. It's about Tegan and the way heat simmered inside me when he teased about being hot. The way my heart sped up and my stomach dropped at the same time. More than anything, it's about the split second before accidental contact between my fist and his face, where I wanted to believe he could really think I'm hot.

I know I'm not ugly. Really I do. Like I said, I know I have a decent face. I'm not the girl who sits around being down on herself all the time. But I'm also a realist; I don't see flowers and rainbows where they aren't. I know boys and I know what they think of as hot. I'm not their definition. Which is why the whole Billy situation pisses me off so much. Things weren't how they seemed, but of course, I'm the one who came out looking like the desperate girl who thought a guy like him would want her.

The difference here is, with Tegan, I had that second of wanting it to be true. A girl's allowed a second of insanity, right? And to make sure it doesn't become more than that second, I skip my next gym day and the one after that. I spend those hours being angry at myself. Can you say self-sabotaging behavior? I can, but it doesn't stop me from doing it. Over and over again until it's been a week since my last day at the gym and I've totally blown my eating plan. All that hard work is wasted. Sometimes I eat because I'm stressed. So sue me.

The chance to show Billy I'm not the girl he can torture anymore. To show Mom I can be what she wants. I'm blowing it all because of Tegan. All of it down the drain. I've never been as pissed at myself as I am now.

I pull out my old roller blades and contemplate a trip around the park. That's exercise. Not the same as what I do with Tegan, but it would be something. Instead I toss them back in the closet. I text Em only to find out she's in class. Without much of an idea as to where I'm going, I grab my keys. Mom's going to be home early today and the thought of seeing her makes my chest feel tight with guilt.

My feet take the stairs as quickly as they can. The house suddenly feels suffocating with all its memories on the walls and thoughts of dinners past with my parents at the table, the quiet little arguments they have over me like I'm not sitting three feet away.

I jerk the door open and run outside, only to slam into something hard enough that I stumble backward. If it wasn't for the hands that reach out for me, I'd be on my jean covered butt right now.

"Slow down there, Rocky. You're supposed to save that for the gym. If you hadn't missed the past week, that is."

Tegan's hands on me invoke all sorts of feelings I don't want to discuss. Some of them anger, the others...not so much. I step out of his grasp, but all I come up with to say is, "Rocky?"

"Yep. You have a killer hook. Though we're going to have to work on your aim a bit. You were a little off target, but I think with some practice, you'll be knocking people out rather than just giving little black eyes in no time." Tegan looks at me, obviously amused.

Without meaning to, I laugh. There's something about his attitude that's contagious. I want to trust everything he says, laugh at his jokes and even get a flash of myself running up and down those stairs like Sylvester Stallone did in one of the movies. I wonder if it's real. If he's really this happy and those glimpses I get of his secretive side are just that—little blips of time in his life. Or if that's the real Tegan and he tries to hide it with his playfulness.

My mind is spending way too much time on this guy. I realize I'm screwed, so I take another step backward and cross my arms. All it does is give me a better view of his deep brown penetrating eyes. There's something so real about them. Even though he looks like all the Billy Masons out there, he might be different.

Pretty boys have this power to make girls crazy and if I don't stop thinking about the realness in his eyes, I have a feeling I'm heading to padded cell territory. "Whatever. Being smooth isn't going to make this better."

Tegan holds his hands up. "You're not going to hit me again, are you? I knew I should have grabbed an ice pack."

Damn him for forcing me to fight a smile. "I'm going now." When I try to push the door closed, Tegan sticks his foot out to stop it.

This time, he's serious when he speaks. "Five minutes."

I nod my head yes at him, already feeling a crack in my defenses.

"Listen, maybe this is me being a total guy here, but I have no clue what I did to piss you off. Mom says guys are kind of dense when it comes to girls so I'm assuming this is one of those times. The only thing I can come up with is I made you uncomfortable and that freaks me out. I really wasn't going for sexual harassment when I said that—"

"Aw, so that's why you're here. You're worried about your job. Don't worry. I'm not going to tell them you harassed me." I hate to admit it stings a little. Deep down, I wanted there to be another reason he came. Maybe it's just because I actually had a little fun with him, but like I thought, it's all just a job to him.

Tegan pushes his hair out of his face. "This is the second time you've said that. Your money is no better than anyone else's. I wouldn't be here if that were the case."

"Why are you here?"

He shrugs. "I didn't like the way we left things. You're my client. I take my job seriously."

Ouch. His answer hurts worse than it should.

"Plus... I owe you, I guess."

It just keeps getting worse. First I'm his job and then a favor. "I helped you get a chair out of a car, Tegan. It's not like I came up with a cure for cancer or something."

"I don't like to owe people."

"It's called kindness. Again, it wasn't a big deal."

"It's a big deal to me." The finality in his tone tells me he's done and I am too.

"Okay, fine then. Tell me how you know where I live?"

He looks down at the ground for a second. When his head rises, he's kind of looking up at me, a mischievous smile on his face. "You've got two things on me, Annabel Lee: harassment and stealing your address off your record."

"Ugh!" I gasp, not really sure what to say.

"Breaking the rules is a little fun. I promise, I don't do it as much as I used to though."

"You used to steal girl's addresses a lot? God! Maybe I should turn you in, Stalker Boy." I can't believe I'm joking around with him. No, what I can't believe is how fun it is.

His face pales. "No! That's not what I meant. Yours is the only address or phone number I've ever taken. I meant breaking the rules. Gives you a little rush, ya know?"

"Are you mental?" This boy is all kinds of confusing. I'm not sure I know up from down when I'm around him.

Tegan laughs. "That's one of the things I like about you. You say what's on your mind. Plus, you're funny. Not sure you really see it though."

This time I don't fight my laugh. In fact, I hardly even cover my mouth when it bursts free. It takes a few minutes before I settle down enough to speak. "Me? I say what's on my mind? Not even close. No one in my life knows how I really feel about anything."

"Hmm, maybe I'm just special then. Do you have a crush on me, Annabel Lee?" There's laughter in his voice, but my insides freeze. This is not happening again.

"Okay, I can tell from your face I just screwed up again, but I'm not sure how. Can we skip to the part where you tell me, so I can apologize and ask you to come back to the gym? You make things a lot more interesting around there."

My body starts to heat. "Oh, just because you're gorgeous you think you can get away with whatever you want. That you'll ask me to come back to the gym and I'll just do it. Well think again, buddy!"

66

"You think I'm gorgeous?" It's not a real question. He's only trying to frustrate me.

"Ugh! I hate you!" I try and slam the door, but he stops me again. His eyes go from flirty to serious in T minus two seconds.

"I'm not playing games. I'm not sure why you think that."

"Um, because look at me and look at you. You know my percentage of body fat for God's sake. You can't know that kind of information and then tease about my hit being hot or tell me I make the gym more interesting. I get the rules and I'm okay with them. Don't try and make me look stupid. I can't workout with you." The words stick in my mouth like cotton candy. I want to work out. I want to work out with Tegan too.

But then I get annoyed again when he actually steps inside my doorway to keep me from closing the door on him. "There are so many things I want to say about what you just said, but I'm going to focus on the workouts. If you want this, really want it, don't fight it just because you don't like me. Get another trainer. Keep me. Whatever, but don't lose faith." He shrugs. "If you really want this that is."

His words sound suspiciously like a challenge to me and by the way half his mouth twitches, I can tell it is. I want to fight it, fight him, but there's a bigger part of me who wants to take him up on this. Not just because it *is* what I want, but because there's something about him that intrigues me. I'd never admit it to anyone but myself, but I need to know what makes him tick. Why he's so freaked out about getting help from people, when it's obvious he puts himself out there for everyone else.

"Just say yes, Rocky. I know you're going to. I watched you that first day. Saw the determination on your face while you walked to the gym. Then you'd let it beat you a little. Totally different body language while you walked back to your car."

Not sure how I feel about him studying my body language.

"Then your head would be held high again when you'd walk back. Show me that determination. Show me what I saw on your face when you were hitting that punching bag."

I lean against the door, knowing I have no defense for him. "You're determined."

"Show me you're more determined."

I just don't get it. All his answers sound so real. They make sense when he says them, but I really don't get why he'd come all the way here, go through this much trouble just for me. "Why?" I ask again. It takes him a minute to reply. When he does, I know he really understood what I meant.

His eyes divert from mine, studying something on my house. "You were pissed that first day. You wanted to kick my ass, but then you saw...and you helped. No matter how you felt about me you did it because it was the right thing to do. Not because you felt sorry for anyone. It was just a reflex."

His words almost steal mine. They do capture my breath. "Anyone would have."

He shakes his head. "No, they wouldn't."

More bits and pieces of him start to show. Who wasn't there for him? Who shattered his belief in people helping him or his family?

Tegan's eyes find mine. The way he's looking at me, it's like he can see through me. As though he knows things about me no one else does. I want to see what he does. "Yeah, okay. Just...don't play games with me, kay? Be real."

Tegan nods.

"So, tomorrow?" I ask.

———

69

"It's our day of—oh wait, I picked up a few extra hours, but not till later. Go jogging with me."

Automatically, I want to say no, but then I remember the decision I just made. The one I'm sticking with no matter what. "Okay, but I'm warning you, there is no way I'll be able to keep pace with you."

Tegan smiles and steps back on the porch. "Don't doubt yourself, Annabel Lee. You can do it. I'll pick you up tomorrow at 6:00 AM."

"WHAT?"

He tilts his head and gives me a look. "Wussing out already?"

"Ugh, fine. See you at six." Then I remember Mom and Dad. "Um, can we meet though?"

He looks a little offended before telling me to meet him at Let's Get Physical instead. He gets halfway down my walkway before turning to face me again. "I'm probably going to regret this, but remember, you promised to be there." He's quiet for a second and then says, "And I am…looking, I mean. You said look at you and I just want to tell you, I am."

Then he's gone and I'm left more out of breath than any treadmill or round of boxing could ever leave me.

**

I'm standing in front of my mirror in a pair of pajama bottoms and a t-shirt. It's ridiculous, I know. I see myself every day, but I can't help but study every rounded curve of my body. No inch goes unnoticed. My shiny black hair, the freckles on my nose. My eyes, like I said, I've always liked those. My mouth isn't bad either, I don't think. Plump lips are in right? I mean, ever since Angelina Jolie at least.

There's a little mole by my collar bone. A dimple on the right side of my mouth when I smile big. I frown. It's much smaller that way.

He said he's looking. Tegan's looking at *me* and I'm trying to figure out what he sees. I know what I see. There's little dimple in my thigh, resting under my rear. My arms are too big. Is that what he sees? If so, why is he looking?

Turning to the side, I suck in my stomach. My boobs aren't bad. Actually, I'm pretty proud of them. They're nice and round. Much bigger than Em's, but not too big, if you ask me. She always says she wishes hers were more like mine. Are they what he sees?

Or is that not what he meant at all? That he's looking deeper than what he sees on the outside? My willingness to help him with his brother seems big to him. Like it actually meant something. Like it tells him something about me. Maybe I'm studying myself in the mirror for nothing and it's really the helpful girl who pulled a chair from a van that he's talking about.

I want both to be true. I like being seen for the inside, but for once, I'd love for someone to look at me too. To think I'm beautiful, not in the "you'd-have-a-pretty-face-but" way that I'm used to.

I think of Em again, the need to call her, to tell her surging inside me. She's my best friend and she'll support this. She'll support me, right? And she'll always be honest. I need to know exactly what she thinks when she looks at me.

Turning for my cell, I jump when I see a figure standing in my doorway. "Mom. You scared the bejesus out of me."

Her arms are crossed in another suit. It's almost bedtime and she hasn't changed yet. "What were you doing?"

My tongue itches to tell her. To really ask her what she thinks about me, but I'm scared of the answer. "Nothing." I shrug.

I turn back to the mirror and she comes up and steps behind me. "I've been thinking…"

"What?"

She fingers my hair. "How would you like a few highlights? It might be fun to do something different, don't you think?"

Actually, I kind of like my hair. I didn't realize it until this second. "Maybe…"

"We can make a day of it. Have a spa day. Manicures, pedicures. There's a new shop in town I've thought about making an appointment at. They specialize in clothes that help…they're slimming, accentuating your assets."

When I look in the mirror now, I don't see the boobs I'd been admiring moments ago. My eyes don't look as blue and now my lips just feel fat, not like kissable rosebuds. I'm thinking about the dimple in my thigh. The stomach that's anything but flat. I even forget the girl who helped Tegan because it was the right thing to do.

"Sure."

But really I wonder why Tegan bothers looking.

Chapter Six

DOUBLE THE REJECTION

I'm wearing a pair of gray sweats and a black t-shirt when I pull up to Let's Get Physical at ten minutes to six. In the passenger seat is my backpack with a change of clothes, just a simple pair of capris, one of those shirts with the tie underneath my boobs and sandals. Not sure why I brought them, but figured the last thing I would want is to be in need of something other than sweats and not have it on-hand.

I turn off my car and fiddle with my keys while waiting for Tegan to get here. It's so crazy, being here and waiting for him to go jogging. I haven't jogged for fun in—wow, I can't even remember. And now I'm doing it with my trainer? What was I thinking?

Shaking my head, I fight to stamp down my doubt. He won't push me too hard. That I can tell about him. He's good at his job. Understanding and encouraging, which is what I need. Even if he is a little cocky and moody some of the time.

Picking up my cell phone, I glance at the time. 6:10. Nerves start a slow boil in my belly. Not everyone can be on time all the time. Especially at six in the morning.

—

74

Shoving my keys back into the ignition, I give power to the car to listen to music. I wonder where we're going to run. Hopefully it's not someplace that's packed with people. For some reason, I think Tegan knows better than that though. I'm sure he knows I'm a total wuss and it would make me uncomfortable.

I glance up to see a few people walk into Let's Get Physical. What if he's waiting inside? I didn't even think about that. For the second time I turn off my car before heading inside. He's not standing by the door, but Supermodel is sitting behind the desk.

"Hi, Annabel. You here to do a solo workout today?" She asks.

Her words pretty much answer my question, but I ask anyway. "Is Tegan around?"

"No, not that I've seen."

Thanking her, I walk out. The nerves start to bubble over now, a rapid boil like right before you toss noodles into the water. It's only 6:25. He wouldn't have asked me to come if he didn't plan to show up, right?

75

I climb back into my car because the last thing I want to do is stand here on the street waiting for him. I try the radio, nothing is on. Hit play on my CD player, but then turn it off because I'm not in the mood to change the CD. Immediately, I reach for my phone: check my email, look for a text from Em, change the wallpaper.

Finally, the boil bubbles over, spilling throughout my body. 7:00. He's not here. He's not coming. What was I thinking? Shaking my head, I toss my cell into the passenger seat, start my car and drive off.

I don't bother to grab my bag when I get home. I'm half afraid I'll chuck the dumb thing across my lawn. Maybe he asked me to run with him to pacify me. To look like he actually cared, knowing that I'd be too proud to back down after I promised him I'd keep working out. But that doesn't feel real. Doesn't feel like him.

I lean my head forward so my forehead presses against my front door. What am I thinking? I don't know this guy. Actions speak louder than words. His actions spoke pretty loudly.

My door pulls open and I stumble to catch myself. I'm so shocked to see my mom on the other side of the door, that when she asks me what I'm doing, I answer honestly. "I went jogging." Okay, maybe not completely honestly since I didn't actually jog, but I'd planned on it.

Doubt is written all over her face. "You went jogging?"

I stand taller. "Yes."

She looks at me for a minute, as if she's trying to figure me out. Should she be happy or not? Believe me or not? "I don't like you out and about without being honest with me about what you're doing. I'll let it go this time, but next time, try the truth." She checks her cell phone, grabs her keys, and the urge to grab them out of her hand and throw them the way I just thought about throwing my bag takes over.

"I'm not lying. Thanks for the vote of confidence though."

She sighs. Her colored-in brows pull together. "I'm not trying to be a monster here, but you don't look like you've been exercising. You look rested. You're not sweating and this may sound harsh, but I've never seen you get up this early and go for a jog before." She steps outside. "I'm running late. We'll talk about it later."

And then she's gone and I'm left feeling even worse than I did waiting on a boy who never came.

—

"Scoot over." Em plops on my bed beside me. Her ever-present hoodie is laid across my computer chair. The only time she doesn't wear it is at home, or in my room. Even the teachers let her wear it during PE. She has a copy of Edgar Allen Poe poetry on her lap. She's always been into poetry, reading and writing. While I like it, I usually don't read the same kind of things she does. I'm more of a paranormal romance kind of girl. Sad... I know, but if a girl and a fallen angel can fall in love? I guess that gives a girl hope.

Or at least a few hours of quality entertainment.

"How did things go at the doctor?" I ask. Her mom is always bringing her to see specialists about her birthmark. It's different than the way my mom is about my weight though. I know Ms. M does it because even though Emily will never admit it, she wants it gone. More than anything, Em wishes she could make it disappear.

She's such a contradiction. She hides behind her hoods and hair, but then goes on about how she doesn't care what other people think. Wants to disappear, but will draw attention to herself to defend me. Pretends to not care about the mark, rolls her eyes at her mom when they make another doctor's appointment, but really hope ignites in her eyes.

She drops the book onto her lap. We're both lying on our backs, knees bent. "Same old thing. I don't know why Mom's always dragging me to the appointments."

Her words spark visions of the gym. Of Tegan. I push him aside, because I don't want to think about him. Not about how it felt when he bailed on me. I'm going to the gym for me and it has nothing to do with Mr. No show.

But my working out and her doctor appointments are kind of the same thing, aren't they? We're both going to try and change the things that seem to define us. I know the real answer to my question and I know what she will say, but I ask anyway. "Don't you want to go though? I mean, just to see?"

Em sighs. "Why? So I can fit in with people like Billy Mason? They're assholes and they'll keep looking for a reason to put people a step below them."

I immediately feel foolish, because the main reason I'm doing what I'm doing is because of people like him. Because I want to show them I'm more than they think I am. "Yeah, but you'd have to admit, it'd be nice to shock them, ya know? Show them we're just as good as they are." Show my mom I'm not a liar and that I'm as good as she is too.

Em rolls over to face me. "But it won't. People in general are jerks. That's why I don't like anyone but you and my mom. There are certain people who will always be the ones getting stepped on and those who will always do the stepping. That's the way the world works, Bell. Crappy, but true."

I don't believe her. I can't. What's the point of it all if that were true? But what if I'm lying to myself and I really believe it? I'd thought just like her the first time I saw Tegan. I turned out to be right about him too. There's a part of me who fights to share her beliefs. "I don't know about that."

"And that's why we fit together so well. Why we'll always be best friends. You're the softie while I'm the hard-nosed bitch. See? Perfect." And then she sits up and smacks me with a pillow.

"Ugh, you *are* a bitch." I roll off the bed, grab a pillow and hit her with it in retaliation. Before I know it, we're laughing like crazy and smacking each other with my pillows. Somehow Em helps me forget about Mom and Tegan.

"You're going down, Malone." I take a swing at her, but when I do, she rips the pillow out of my hand and starts hammering me with hers. I fall to the bed. "You're such I cheater! I give up." Em falls down beside me again, laughing, free in a way she isn't very often. It makes me sad for her.

"I always win, Bell. Remember," she points to herself, "hard-nosed bitch." I shake my head, her words swimming around inside my ears.

"It sucks… People, I mean."

"I know, but at least you have me." Emily laughs, making me laugh too.

"You're right. Who needs those jerks?" And I'll show Tegan. I'll show up at the gym like nothing happened. Maybe I'll pretend I didn't show too. And Mom? My chest pinches. No matter what, I will always want her to love me. I will never stop fighting for that.

Right about then, my cell vibrates with a text. I pull it out and look. "Mom's home. Come on. You're staying for dinner." After what happened this morning, I need Em's support. I just hope and pray she doesn't say anything about my jog this morning.

"I can't believe your mom texts you from downstairs for dinner." Em pulls her hoodie on as we're walking out of my room. "Even worse, I can't believe you're making me eat with her."

"What are best friends for?" I bump her hip as we go down the stairs. Dad is sitting in his spot, slacks and t-shirt, while Mom looks like she's at a business dinner. You know, the typical night around the Conway household.

"Hey, kiddo. I didn't know you were here." Dad gives Em his infectious smile and she returns it. He's actually another person she can add to her list of people she trusts, though I'm not sure she'd admit it to me.

Mom, on the other hand, paints that fake smile on her face. It's not like she reserves it for Em specifically. I get it all the time too. A lot of people do because she'd never cause a scene about anything. Always smiling.

"Emily. I didn't know you were joining us."

"Yep." Before anything can go wrong, I say. "Let's go get your plate, Em." A few minutes later we're back in the dining room with her utensils. Sitting on the table a lasagna, salad and bread sticks. Not homemade mind you. Dad probably picked it up on his way home, but cooked in the kitchen or a restaurant, I'm positive this isn't on my meal plan. At least not very much of it.

I love Italian. It's my favorite.

Dad takes a helping, and passes it to me. It looks so good. Smells so good, the sweet basil tickling my nose, and I want to indulge, but I don't. I cut myself a tiny square of the cheesy goodness. Maybe an inch by an inch. I haven't been keeping track of my calories like I should, partially because I spent a whole week sabotaging myself.

But Tegan also talked about portion control. Not denying myself, but limiting myself. Something about this not being a diet, but a lifestyle change. This tiny square is probably equal to or less than Mom will eat, so why am I feeling guilty?

"You okay over there?" Em snaps me out of my lasagna analysis.

I smile at her. "Shut up." And then I hand her the dish. She takes a piece about triple mine. Em was blessed with nice metabolism. I skip out on the bread sticks and scoop a little more salad than I usually would on my plate. Vegetables have never really been my favorite, but during a lifestyle change, vegetables are my friend.

My eyes find Mom. She looks at my plate, then at me and smiles. It's a real smile and I can't help but return it. Somehow my plate has overpowered my fake run this morning.

"Wow. I brought home lasagna special and that's all you're going to have? I'm crushed." Dad winks at me.

"Daniel, don't. There's nothing wrong with her plate. You're pushing bad habits onto her."

"I didn't say there was anything wrong with it. I was making conversation. Teasing our daughter."

Em squeezes my knee under the table, knowing how much I hate it when they argue about me. "Well, I know I'm starved. I can't wait to eat the lasagna, Dr. C."

"Don't you eat all my food. I'm going back for seconds." Dad's teasing breaks the mood. I use the light dressing on my salad, thankful Mom buys it anyway so I didn't have to ask for it. Soon we're all concentrating on our food and not playing, 'dissect Annabel's meal.'

"So, Emily. Did Annabel tell you what we're doing?"

My fork clanks against my plate. I scramble to pick it up. Both Dad and Em's eyes are on Mom. And I know I'm screwed because I know what she's going to say and I know how Em's going to feel.

"No, she didn't Ms. Conway."

Mom claps her hands together. "Oh. It's so exciting. We're going out for a girl's spa day. She wants to get her hair and nails done. And shopping of course. There are clothes out there to help enhance almost any figure and—"

84

"Why does her figure need enhanced?" Em's voice is tense.

Dad adds, "She *wants* to do all this? If she does, I'm all for it. I just want to be sure it's something she really wants."

Yep. I'm definitely screwed.

"Why wouldn't she, Daniel?" Mom asks.

"I'm still trying to figure out why she has to find clothes to enhance anything when she's perfect the way she is," Em says.

"All girls want to maximize their assets and hide their imperfections."

Em blanches at Mom. "I don't!"

"Wait a minute. What assets are we drawing attention to here?" Dad breaks in. I feel dizzy as their words all run laps around me. All three of them, trying to talk for me. All of them thinking they know what's best for me. All of them making me feel smaller and smaller. Unfortunately, not in the good way.

"Paulette, you're always doing this!"

"I'm only trying to help!"

"You're perfect the way you are, Bell," Em says from beside me.

Suddenly the food isn't sitting so well in my stomach. That same anger from my boxing day is begging to burst free, until I can't hold it back any longer. I shove myself up from the table. "Stop it! All of you, just stop it!" The room is dead silent as six eyes are on me. "I can't do this. I don't need you all arguing about me like everyone knows what's best for me. Just…just back off. Right now I just need all of you to back off."

Part of me feels bad for leaving Em, but I can't stay. On my way out the door, I grab my keys and purse and I'm gone. With no clue where to go, I drive. Drive and drive until I'm sitting at a stop sign by the middle school. There's a track right behind it.

I jerk into the parking lot, park and head straight for the track. I'm not wearing the right shoes. I have on capris, but I don't care. I don't need Mom. I don't need Tegan. I get out and run. My legs ache. My lungs burn, but I make myself jog the whole lap. It's still freeing. Like each of my steps is healing me from my day. Like *I'm* healing *me* by doing something. When I make the whole loop I fall into the grass and die. Okay, not really, but I feel like it. But it feels good too. I just did something incredible.

CHAPTER SEVEN

A MOTHER'S HUG

I return Tegan's smile when I walk into the gym. "What are we doing first?" Instead of waiting for him to reply, I keep walking through the gym. Luckily my voice doesn't sound as annoyed as I really am. I'm still hurt he no showed on me.

He steps up beside me. "Cardio, like always."

This time it's me who leads the way to the machines. *I can do this. I can do this.* I'm not even sure how many times I say the words, trying to make them true. It's not as easy as I thought it would be to pretend I don't care, that I expected more of him and he let me down.

It's me who pushes the buttons to get my tread going today. I fall into a slow jog, without waiting to see what Tegan will do. Again, he climbs on his own machine beside me. We jog in silence for ten minutes and forty-five seconds. Stupid timer.

"I know you're mad. I planned on coming. Something just came up."

Something came up? *Something came up?!* Boys suck. So I ignore him for two minutes and ten seconds. "Something came up? I know you stole my phone number. You used my address, you could have used my number too."

"I know."

He knows? Now I'm even more annoyed. My legs speed up and I'm jogging faster. "Well, glad to hear you know. Too bad I wasn't worthy of the call you knew how to make." Part of me knows I shouldn't be making this big a deal of it. He owes me nothing, but I can't help it. Somehow he made me expect something and didn't follow through.

"It was important." His voice is soft, but firm.

"Oh? And what was so important. I *waited* for you Gym Boy."

"Shit." He steps off the treadmill. "I wanted to be there. We have work to make up for and…It was important," he says again, but still not telling me where he was. Somehow, I know he won't.

We have work to make up for. Did I really expect the jog to have been about anything else? It still stings. "You know what? I don't care. Let's just finish our workout."

I step off the machine. Tegan walks away and I follow. We go through our routine. Abdominals, which let me tell you, is super embarrassing. Today's an arm day so he walks me through a bunch of arm exercises. He only talks to tell me how many repetitions to do or to urge me on. I only talk when I have to, which thankfully isn't very often.

The whole time I can't stop thinking about sitting in that car. His non-answer. The apology he never offers. Or the fact that somehow, I let myself believe he actually wanted to spend time with me when really he only wanted to make up for a workout. Still, I keep searching for an answer, or hoping there is one.

"Good workout today." Tegan crosses his arms and leans against the building. This is the first time he's actually walked me out of the building.

"Thanks," I mumble, pulling my keys out of my bag. Then I start to walk away.

"Hey," he calls out to me and idiotically I stop. "I'm sorry."

And then it hits me. I'm not sure why I realize it now, but I think I know why he didn't come. Timidly, I turn. "You were with your brother, weren't you? You were helping out with something." If it's true, it doesn't excuse why he didn't call. It really doesn't explain why he didn't just tell me the truth, but it makes the not-showing-up part kind of okay.

Tegan's eyes don't tell me anything. They're wide and staring straight at me. He hasn't moved. I'm not even sure he's breathing right now.

"It's okay… I mean, if that's the reason, it's okay. I understand."

Finally he moves, pushing away from the wall slightly. "Why? Because I'm the guy with the crippled brother? That excuses me for everything?" Tegan shakes his head, his blond hair blowing gently in the slight breeze. "See you next time, Annabel Lee." Turning around, he heads back for the building. I don't know where the courage comes from, but when anger bursts to the surface, I let it out.

"You know what? It's not okay! You're right. Even if you were helping your brother it doesn't give you the right to no call no show!"

He turns like my yelling surprises him. It surprises me too. I don't wait for his reply though. I turn and walk away.

***

"Annabel, wake up. I need your help." Mom's voice first thing in the morning is never a good thing. Nothing would please me more than to roll over and pretend I'm still sleeping, but then, that wouldn't work with her would it? Maybe another mom, but not mine.

"Yeah?" I sit up and rub my eyes.

"We had a cancelation and I need your help with a few things to get ready for the pageant."

It's even worse than I thought. Is it possible for me to lie back down and play dead? "Isn't there anyone else?"

"No there's not. That's why I'm here. It's not as if I ask you for a lot, Annabel."

No, not a lot at all. Just perfection. "Okay, I'll be down in ten." She closes the door and I get out of bed and get ready. The car ride is practically silent. I don't know what I was thinking—riding with her like this. I wonder if she's as nervous as I am. Me because I don't want to see the beauty queens from my high school and her because she doesn't want to see me next to the girls. It will only remind us both what we don't have.

When we get there, I waste no time finding a quiet corner to paint. It's a plain backdrop that I have to paint white. Not hard, but Mom has checked on me four times in an hour. Not because she's curious, but because she doubts me. While I paint, Elizabeth and her crew are too cool to bother with me.

Mom and Bridgette are working on a schedule of some sort. They didn't offer me much information and I didn't ask. When I finish the painting I move on to whatever other odd jobs they need me to do. Pull lighting, more props, and chairs from the storage. I've probably sneezed a million times because of the dust. I wonder if anyone else here has allergies like I do?

Just like my workout with Tegan the other day, Mom only talks to me when she has to. It's not to be mean either. I know that. This is her element. She's ordering people around and planning something big. Something that will make everyone say, "Wow, look what Paulette Conway did." I don't fit into the equation.

And Elizabeth and crew? They just stay away from me. They're too cool to want anything to do with me.

Finally, when I've done everything on Mom's list, I hunt to find her, hoping we can leave. Following the hallway back stage, I head toward the offices, stopping when I hear my name.

"What about Annabel? Would she be interested in taking Ella's place? I'm sure the two of you could throw something together in time, Paulette."

It's a woman's voice. I'm not sure who. I know it isn't Bridgette. I'm sure she'd know better than to ask.

"No, pageants aren't really Annabel's thing. She's made it clear she wouldn't want to participate."

I had? Holy moly. When did I start making things clear that I never knew about? I mean, I'd rather poke my own eyes out, but I never told her that.

Or maybe not, maybe if she'd ask, I'd surprise both of us and want to do it with her.

"You never know. We're kind of in a bind here. Maybe you could ask her."

Ask me... Don't ask me... Ask me... Don't ask me... I don't want to participate, but I want her to want me to. Just this once.

"She has plans, Evelyn. It wouldn't work out. She's going to be out of town with her friend Emily that night." She's not going to ask me. My eyes start to sting.

94

"Darn. I'll figure something out. Thanks for everything, Paulette." Footsteps sound as I assume Evelyn walks away.

"Is she really going out of town?" Bridgette asks.

"Of course not. I can't let her embarrass herself like that, Bridge. You know it would be a disaster."

What I hear is, embarrass me like that. I squeeze my eyes shut, not allowing myself to cry and then I walk out. The second I get outside I remember I don't have my car with me. Nice. What am I supposed to do now?

Mine and Em's favorite coffee shop is only a block away so I head there. Once I have a coffee—crap, water in me. Stupid diet. Hopefully water will do the trick and help me relax. Then maybe I can call Em to see if she can pick me up. We haven't seen each other in a few days.

One water bottle later, two familiar people come in. Tegan's mom and brother. I freeze, like it will somehow make me disappear.

They order their drinks and then look around the busy shop. There are no empty tables. In fact, the only empty seats are the ones by me. My stomach feels like I just had a triple shot and nothing to eat all day, but I wave at them. "Hi. I don't know if you remember me, but I helped you guys at the gym the other day."

Tegan's mom smiles and as his brother wheels himself over. "Of course I remember you! That was so nice of you to help. I'm sorry I didn't get to thank you that day, but I turned around and you were gone."

I give them a smile. "It was no big deal. I'm about to head out though. I just wanted to tell you guys you could have my table if you want it."

"Sit. You're not going anywhere, but we'll join you."

Automatically, my butt falls into the chair. It's not in the way I would sit if Mom told me to, but in a way that I want to sit.

"We have a couple hours to kill while they work on the lift for the van. We could use a little company…"

"Annabel." It's an instant like. There's something so friendly and welcoming about his mom.

"I'm Dana and this is Timmy."

"Tim, Ma. I swear, you and Tegan treat me like I'm a baby."

She ruffles his hair. "Aw, my little Timmy-wimmy-kins." He shoves her hand away, cheeks red.

"Whatever."

I feel warm inside watching them. "Nice to meet you." I look at Tegan's bother. "Nice to meet you too, Tim."

He beams at me. "Do you play Gin Rummy? I kick Mom and Tegan's butt. I need some real competition."

Like his brother, he makes me laugh. They remind me of each other. The same brown eyes, blond hair and he has Tegan's same smile. His real one, not the Ken smile. "You're on."

We play four games. I'm not sure I ever laughed so hard in my life. Tim and his mom joke with each other, tease each other. They're happy in a way mom has never been with me. When she looks at him, you see how much she loves him. She sees more than his chair in a way Mom will never see more than my weight.

There are so many times they talk about Tegan where it would be so easy for me to ask about him. To try and find out which Tegan is real. I'm sure I can even find out what they did the other day, but I don't. None of it feels right.

A good two hours pass before Tegan's mom's cell phone rings and they let her know the van is ready. On autopilot I slump back in my chair. Not only do I not want to go home, I haven't called Em yet.

"Do you need a ride home?" Tim's eyes are wide, excited when he asks.

The urge to say yes almost overpowers me. "I'm going to call my friend to pick me up. Thanks anyway."

97

"Are you sure? Any girl who gives my brother a black eye is a friend of mine."

My cheeks heat. "It was an accident! I swear I didn't mean to hit him." My eyes find Dana, but she's only laughing.

"Don't worry, sweetie. I'm sure he deserved it. Plus, he was pretty proud of that black eye." She answers.

"Proud?"

"Yep. You made him proud. He couldn't stop bragging about the girl who gave him a right hook."

My breath catches. I don't think she notices because suddenly she's hugging me goodbye. I hug her back tightly, wondering what it would feel like for Mom to give me hugs this strong.

"Thanks for hanging out with us." She winks at me and then she and Tim are gone.

***

I'm lying in bed, my room dark. I've been trying to go to sleep for hours, but it's just not happening. I roll to the left and think about Tegan, how he doesn't like to talk about his brother. The family that obviously loves him and who, by the way they were talking, they're all incredibly close.

About how his mom said he couldn't stop talking about me, even though it was only about my punch.

Roll to the right and I think about her hug. How accepting she was to me, even though we hardly know each other. She hugged me the way Dad does.

On my back I think about Mom. How much I embarrass her. It kills me to embarrass her. I don't understand why, when she doesn't even care enough to have thanked me for helping today. She asked why I disappeared, easily accepted my lie about Em and then went on and on about the pageant she wants me to have nothing to do with.

When my phone vibrates on my bedside table, I jump. Rolling over I pick it up. It's a text, but I don't know the number.

Hey. It's Tegan.

Why is he texting me? Why do my hands shake when I reply? **Hey.**

I'm sorry for being an ass.

It's not okay. My bravery makes me smile.

I'm glad… meet me tomorrow? Same time, same place. I promise to show up this time.

Meet him? I don't know if I can… I don't know if I can't. I want to know more about him and for some reason, I want him to know more about me too. **How do I know you're not going to ditch me?**

I'll be there. Scouts honor. The question is, will you?

It takes me ten minutes to reply. **Yes.**

Chapter Eight

A JOGGING WE WILL GO

To my surprise, Tegan stands next to a beat up Honda Accord when I pull up in front of Let's Get Physical, smoothie in hand. This time, I'm not early. Who cares if I had to park around the corner and wait until I could drive up at the exact right time?

I pretend to fiddle with my bag to buy myself a minute. This time our jog is really going to happen and it freaks me out. Makes me realize a part of me was glad he didn't show last time.

When I look up, Tegan is standing right by my window. He taps his wrist and I get out of the car. "What? We're not jogging from *here* are we?" The thought of people out for their morning coffee seeing my jigglies is not my idea of fun.

"No, get in. I'm driving." He's wearing a pair of basketball shorts and a t-shirt, his elusive tattoo still hiding from view.

I glance at my car and back at him. It's not like I mind him driving, but like I said, this isn't the best side of town so I'm a little nervous about leaving my car here.

"It'll be okay, princess. Don't worry about it. I already told Kim to keep an eye out for you, not that I need to."

I bite my cheeks so I don't smile. Reaching over, I grab my backpack and water bottle, lock up and walk over to his car. My backpack is strategically in front of me, which is lame. I can't hide behind it and I'm not sure why I'm trying.

My pack follows me to my lap when I sit in the passenger side. I wrap my arms around it, holding it tight. A second later, Tegan's behind the wheel.

"I'm not going to bite, ya know. You'd think you were the one who almost got knocked out with how freaked out you look over there."

It happens automatically and I don't realize I've playfully smacked his arm until I've already done it. "I didn't almost knock you out. Stop making me feel bad."

"Whatever you say, Rocky." He looks at me and winks, exactly the way his mom did before pulling away.

We're both quiet. So quiet I fear he might hear my stomach growl. I skipped breakfast this morning, a major no-no on Tegan's list. I really don't get that breakfast is the most important meal of the day crap. "Where are we going?" His tattooed arm is his left so even though I'm pretty sure his sleeve is high enough that I should be able to see it, I can't because it faces his window.

"Right outside of town. There are some trails people jog on. It's real secluded except for the joggers. If you keep going there's a little park out there too. Not real big. Just some picnic tables and stuff. That cool?"

"Um, yeah. Secluded sounds good to me."

Tegan turns his head a little, giving me a really wicked smile. "If you wanted to be alone with me, you just had to ask."

"I-!" have no idea what to say… "You are so conceited!"

"I'm just giving you crap. You make it way too easy. I'm trapped in that gym most of my life and the other girls aren't nearly as fun as you."

My stomach starts to feel queasy and it has nothing to do with skipping out on breakfast. Today he's the light, sarcastic Tegan. "I'm sure I make a much easier mark than them."

He squints his eyes, trying to figure out what I mean and then says, "Hey. That's not what I meant, Annabel Lee. I meant… I guess I just meant I don't have fun with the rest of them. I need a little fun in my life."

Butterflies chase away the nausea. Who knew butterflies could be so fierce? Right now, mine are, because I think he just admitted something that might not have been too easy for him. I shrug and smile. "Thanks?" How stupid. I sound like I'm asking him. "I mean, thanks. Me, too."

———

103

He laughs. "You don't have to lie. I know you're pissed at me half the time. Especially when I ask you somewhere and don't show up…"

I don't know what to say to that so I don't say anything. We're quiet the rest of the way. It doesn't take long before Tegan's pulling his car into an almost deserted lot. The grass behind it is a vivid green and well-trimmed. Little hills dance across the distance, nothing major, but they definitely add to the visual. Trees provide shade, but it's not overbearing. I don't feel like I'm Grisly Adams in the forest or anything. "How did I not know this place was here?"

We get out of the car. "It's pretty much for joggers or bikers. I mean, everyone can come, but not many people do."

"It's beautiful."

"Yep. It's one of my favorite places. We'll see if you still like it after we're done today." Tegan winks at me, before grabbing something out of his trunk and tossing it at me. Luckily I catch it.

"Geez, warn a girl. You could have poked my eye out."

"As opposed to punching it?"

"Whatever." I look at what he handed me. It's some kind of breakfast bar. I raise my eyebrows at him. What is this guy, psychic or something?

"You need to eat to lose weight. Just make sure it's healthy. Plus, you need energy before we head out."

"How'd you…"

"I didn't, but thanks for confirming my suspicion."

This boy is too much! I feel all upside down and backward around him. But the surprising part is, I kind of enjoy it. Not that I'd ever admit it to him. "You suck." Before he can reply I turn so my back is to him and start eating the stupid bar. I hear a package open, telling me he's eating one as well. Tegan offers to take my water bottle for me and before I know it, he's leading me to a path to begin our run. My heart beats about a million miles an hour. My palms are already sweaty and I'm really starting to doubt my own sanity for coming out here with him.

As always, Tegan seems to know. He stops me when we get to the path. "Hey." I turn to face him. He steps toward me and I don't know why, but I gasp. He's so close the butterflies are back in my belly. Why is he so close? His arms reach toward me and I swear I feel like I might pass out and then he's rubbing my arms up and down like my dad would before a pep talk or something. Boys have such an ability to screw with a girl's head. What did I think he would do?

"Relax, Rocky. You're going to knock this out just like you did me."

Why does he insist on bringing this up?

"We're going to take it slow. Jog a bit, walk, jog some more. No biggie. Got it?"

"Got it." And then he's not touching me anymore and jogging away. I ignore the rapid fire beat of my heart and join him. Neither of us talk as we make our way down the path at a slow pace. I'm distinctly aware of him beside me, those soulful eyes of his looking forward. Speaking of forward, maybe I should be looking there too.

So I do. I face the front, trying to focus on nature around us when really all I'm paying attention to is the way our feet pound against the ground to a shared beat. Bump, bump, bump, bump. Our breaths mingle; his mine, his mine. Our own music, and we're playing together without trying. It's then I realize, I like the tune. Maybe a little too much.

"You doing okay over there, Annabel Lee?" You can hardly hear the difference in his voice. He could be lounging on the couch as winded as he sounds.

"Yep." And I am. Sure I feel a little out of breath, and my legs are starting to plead with me to give them a break, but it's not overbearing. It actually feels kind of good.

"Told you, you had this. We'll go a little longer, slow it down to a fast walk and then pick it up again."

This time I only nod in reply. I'm back to our music. The slight rustle of the air in the trees adding a wind section. The way my heart drums, urging me on because this crazy wild rhythm is good for it. And as lame and cheesy as it sounds, it feels freeing. I keep going, keep my focus until Tegan's elbow nudges me.

"Let's take it down a notch."

When he says a notch, that's exactly what he means. This isn't a leisurely stroll.

"You were out there. I'd like to see you tell me you aren't enjoying this. I mean, of course you're enjoying it because I'm here, but the jog too—"

That earns him a sharp smack on the arm. "Ouch!"

"You deserved that. We need to take *you* down a notch."

Tegan turns so he's walk/jogging backward, looking at me. "You like it. Admit you like me teasing you."

"Admit it, you're always fishing for compliments."

"If I admit it, will you?"

"I admit nothing."

"Why doesn't that surprise me?"

It takes a minute to realize what's going on here. Are we flirting? It's such a strange concept. I've never flirted in my life. Maybe that's not what this is. And if it is, it's because Tegan is like that. Kind of flirty. And me? Well I guess I'm getting hypnotized by our music.

"Break over." Before I have a chance to comprehend what he said, he's jogging away and I'm running to try to catch up. It only takes a minute, partly because I somehow find a new burst of energy and also because he slows down for me. We continue on the path doing our walk/jog thing and before I know it, we've made a loop and we're almost back to the car.

There's a burning tingle running the length of my legs. And it sucks. Seriously, it doesn't feel good, but in other ways it does. Like Tegan said, it sort of feels like my war wound. Proof that I've accomplished something.

"We're almost there. Push a little bit more and I'm done torturing you for the day. I swear."

As soon as we make it back to the car, I collapse in the grass. I'm too tired to care how it looks. The air fights to escape me, but I reel it in, taking deep, long breaths until they smooth into a steady rhythm.

Like he'd just woken up from a nap, Tegan hands me my water and sits next to me. He has his hands latched, arms around his legs, feet on the ground in a totally relaxed position. Jerk.

But it's then I realize he just helped me see something I've been way too curious about. The sleeve of his shirt is high enough that I see his sculpted arm and the tattoo on it. It's some kind of symbol. I'm not sure what it means, but then there's a name under it too.

Timmy.

He has a tattoo of his brother's name. It's cool in so many ways, but gives me a ton of questions too. He's so hush, hush when it comes to his brother that the declaration on his arm surprises me.

My heart is no longer beating crazily. It's buried somewhere in my feet.

"Are you checking me out?" he asks, a smile in his voice, only I can't reply. I keep staring at the tattoo. All the dark swirly lines of the design. Each small letter spelling out Timmy's name. Wow... I feel like I'm going to be sick, even though it makes no sense.

"What?" he looks down. "Oh. It means brothers and the other is forever."

"That's cool. I like it."

109

Tegan pushes his hair out of his face. The tense Tegan is back. He's quiet and I'm quiet because I don't know if I should say anything or not. The air around us is thick. It's probably only eight, but I'm feeling hot and not sure it has anything to do with the run I just took. There's something about him that does crazy things to me. I wish I knew how he did it.

It could have been a minute or an eternity before he talks again. It's hard to tell. "You hung out with my family yesterday." He looks at me and there's something different in his eyes. It's not the playfulness, the cockiness or the tenseness. It takes me a moment to realize what it is. It's vulnerability and it steals my breath. So much so I can only nod in reply.

"And you didn't ask about me. Didn't fish for answers. Didn't mention I bailed on you. You just...hung out. Like you wanted to."

There's something that sounds like awe in his voice, like I did something exceptional or something. I'm not exceptional. I'm just me. "Umm, yeah. It was fun. Tim beat me at cards and your mom is incredible."

Another long silence.

"Are they why you're here right now?"

His question confuses me. Little sound bites of our fight pops into my head. When he asked if having a crippled brother excused him. Does he think *I'm* here because I feel sorry for *him?* "No... But I'm still mad at you, too. I mean, there's a part of me who gets it, but another who thinks it's not too much to ask that you picked up a phone."

He turns his head, still sitting in that relaxed position and looks at me. I shiver. He's so beautiful. I shouldn't think that, but I do.

"But you're still here?" There's so much behind his question that I don't understand, but hear it all the same.

"I'm still here." My reply matches the question in his.

A car pulls up in the lot behind us. Just a second later a bike zips by. People are starting to show up and I hadn't noticed. Tegan stands. "Come on. Let's go for a walk." He holds out his hand which is all sorts of strange. I mean, sweet, but strange. I've never had a boy do that before. It reminds me of a movie or something, but I push those thoughts away and let him help me up. When he lets go, I miss his touch.

After we walk a little way, he says, "You also never apologized."

I'm at a loss on what I'm supposed to be apologizing for. Apparently he reads my confusion because he says, "Because I have a handicapped brother. I can't tell you how many times people meet Timmy and then tell me they're sorry."

"It sucks, don't get me wrong, but he seems happy. Well-adjusted and all that."

Tegan huffs which isn't the reply I expect. "He is. Timmy's such a kickass kid. That's what makes it all even worse."

"Yeah—"

Tegan cuts me off before I can finish. "Listen, I just want to apologize again for not showing the other day. Mom needed help with something and I didn't want to say anything because…I guess I'm just fucking sick of it being an excuse for everything, good or bad. People get all weird when it comes to Timmy. They either pity us and walk on eggshells or they don't know how to deal with it at all, so they don't."

It's a link between us I never would have expected. Each of his words spark something inside my heart because I feel the same way. I hate pity. I think about the way he refused my help that first day, the look he gave. "That first day—when I helped—I didn't mean for you to think—"

"No, no." He stops me with his hand. "Okay, maybe kind of, but that was different. The way you just jumped in like that," he shrugs. "It was kind of cool. There wasn't that awkwardness, ya know? Like you felt obligated to help, but then like you thought his paralysis might be contagious at the same time. I hate that."

We start walking again. "Wow, people really act like that?" It's not like he's a leper or something.

"I don't know. Seems like it. Maybe it's just me and I'm too damn sensitive about it." He chuckles.

The urge to admit something to him too plays hide and seek inside me. I want to, but don't know if I can.

"So yeah… thanks. For all of it. The help that day, hanging out with them because you wanted to…And now I'm done. That's about enough of my sob story to last a lifetime."

I take some of his bravery, amazed by how protective he is of his family. "It's not a sob story. I get it…I mean, not in the same way." I study the ground as we walk. "But the pity thing—I get it."

"Who?" he asks.

"Everyone?" My laughter isn't real.

"Who?" he asks again.

How does he know? Maybe the bigger question is can I tell him? "I thought we were done with sob stories?"

"Nope." He shakes his head. "You're not getting out of this. Just this one thing and then we're done." He nudges my arm with his and yes, it makes me a little giddy.

Giddiness had power, because I say, "Two people mostly. A guy from school and—and my mom."

Tegan curses under his breath, but there's no apology. No pity.

"So… how did you end up becoming a trainer?" I'll do anything to change the subject. Plus, there are so many things I still want to know about him. Why does he work so hard? What happened to Tim? Who left them that makes him doubt people want to stick around?

"Timmy. It all leads back to him, doesn't it?" His voice sounds sad. "I just kind of became obsessed with the human body. It really can do amazing, things, Annabel Lee."

There's the name again. I wonder where it comes from.

"It's the only thing to do, and I have to do something, ya know? He's my brother—my family." Tegan picks his cuticle like he's almost nervous. I've never seen him nervous before. "It's my job to take care of him, both of them, but him especially. When I get my degree, I'm going to do whatever it takes to help him walk again."

Something inside me almost...shifts. It's like my eyes have been pried open and I see him. I'm really seeing him for the first time. Not the gorgeous boy, the flirty boy, the one who has girls checking him out left and right at the gym. Not the guy who refuses help or gets edgy when it comes to his brother or his condition. No, I'm seeing the guy who didn't flinch when he saw my weight. Who boxed with me and laughed when I hit him. The guy who would do anything to help people. People like me or people like Tim.

The scary part? The one that makes me want to turn around and jog my big butt to my car and never look back is I realize how much I really like what I see. And that can't be good for me. "Degree?" My voice cracks.

"Physical therapist. College soon. I'm bored of talking about me though. Tell me something about the determined boxing queen that I don't know."

I struggle not to trip. "Ummm. There's not much to tell."

"What? Girls love to talk about themselves, don't they? I'm giving you the prime opportunity." He nudges me again. "I'm good at this, huh?"

Laughter falls out of my mouth. "No, actually, I think you need to be seen by a doctor because there's something wrong with you. Didn't you just tell me the other day you don't understand girls?"

"Damn, I forgot all that honestly from earlier. Now it's screwin' with my game."

My feet glue to the concrete, keeping me from moving. Tegan stops too, giving me one of his confused looks, his eyes searching me, trying to see everything inside me.

"Why do you do that?"

"Do what?" He pushes at that same wayward lock of hair that always falls down in his face.

"The hot stuff at the gym. Say things are messing with your game." As soon as the words come out I pray for the ability to snatch them back, but inside they repeat in my head. Could I say anything lamer? But the fact is, I really need to know.

"I don't know... It's called flirting, I guess. Maybe you've heard of it. It's when a girl or a guy—"

His words give me a rush stronger than our jog just did. My skin burns with heat. Tegan just admitted to flirting with me! "You know what I mean." Despite my shock, I figure I need to push something out of my mouth.

"Actually I don't." He crosses his arms. Frustrated? It almost looks it.

"Tegan..."

Instead of a reply, he glances down at his watch. "I gotta bail. I have to be to work soon. We better head back."

"Are you always working?"

"Eh," he says, but I know the answer is really yes. How many times have I heard about extra shifts?

The walk back to his car is quiet. The drive to the gym, quieter. I hug my backpack, a little bummed that I didn't need the clothes inside. When we get back to Let's Get Physical, he kills the engine. "So, back to our schedule? You're not going to ditch me, right?"

His questions make me smile. I'm actually looking forward to it. "Nope, I'm not going anywhere. Sometimes it might take me a while, but when I decide I'm doing something, I'm doing it."

"I knew that about you. From the beginning I could tell."

Tegan gets out of the car and grabs a gym bag, so I get out too.

"Good job today, Annabel Lee. See you soon." He starts to walk away, but stops. "You're different, you know that? And by the way, I like your eyes." Tegan winks and walks away while I struggle to hide the totally goofy grin plastered to my face. And as much as I'm really craving a celebratory milkshake or even a Berry Berry Blast smoothie, I head home instead.

Chapter Nine

W-DAY AKA WEIGH DAY

It's been the same thing for a week since the incident at the pageant. Mom goes about her business like nothing happened and Dad, not even knowing what the new tension is, tries to make it disappear. Strangely enough, my bright spots have been my workouts with Tegan. Which I guess either makes me lame or someone who might kind of like exercising--at least with him.

My trainer-extraordinaire has been nothing but professional. No more declarations about my eyes, or saying he's flirting with me. Sure, he still runs on the treadmill beside mine, he's still flirtatious with all the girls so even if he was like that with me, it wouldn't mean anything. Which kind of, sort of sucks and it shouldn't.

So maybe it's a good thing he's being professional so my mind won't play tricks on me.

We're trainer and client and even though I've enjoyed our workouts, I'm totally not looking forward to today. There's a heaviness in my chest that won't go away.

Tegan waits for me by the door as always, giving me the smile I'm starting to realize is the real one. Not the Ken smile or the fake one. The Tegan one.

Me, on the other hand, I frown. "How can you be happy on a day like this?"

"It's not that bad, Annabel. You're lucky. You even got to miss a weigh day since you bailed on me for a whole week."

"It's not that bad for *you*. For me, it's torture. I used to weigh every day, and I haven't touched a scale for weeks. Now I'm freaked out about getting on there and finding out I gained five pounds. Of being disappointed I didn't lose anything. *You* have nothing to lose or gain here, no pun intended."

We're back in his little cubby and Tegan puts his hands on my shoulders. He's started to touch me more like this over the last week. Professionally, of course, but still more than he did before. "Relax, Annabel Lee. If it's too much for you, close your eyes and I won't tell you."

"Pfft, like that's going to happen."

He lowers his voice, looking at me with those eyes that seem to see too much. "Then listen to me. Whatever that scales says, you've rocked it this week. Be proud of that, because it's what really matters. You're here and you're doing better every single day."

Wow...he's really good at his job.

I try to turn away, but he hooks a finger under my chin and holds my head in place. I can't turn away, not only because he's touching me and that warm, zapping feeling is flowing from him to me, but because I'm wondering if he can feel any fat on my face.

"I do have something to lose or gain. I'm your trainer, but that's not all. We're... friends, right? I mean, I took a hit for you. Can't sock me in the face and say we aren't friends."

It's annoying how he does this to me, sidetracks me when I'm freaking out. I can't help but smile, some of the heaviness lifting off me in the process. "Are you ever going to stop reminding me of that?"

Tegan drops his hands and gives an easy shrug. "Not when it gets me what I want. You ready for this? I think you're ready."

"Do you always get your way?"

He looks at me like it's a stupid question.

"Ugh, fine. I'm as ready as I'll ever be."

All Tegan says is, "I knew it."

***

"Come on. Show me, Rocky. You're lagging and you know it. You did more repetitions than this last time."

I slide my legs back into place, letting the weights clank extra hard as they snap down. It's easy for him to say. All if this is easy for him. He's not the one who worked his butt off only to realize said butt didn't get any smaller. "My legs are burning."

"That's the point. It's a good burn. That's how you know you're doing something."

I look up at Tegan, trying to silently plead my case. I'm tired, frustrated, fat and done with this for the day, but by the way he crosses his arms, I can tell he won't have any of it. "We have one more set to go, then we can move on. You knock the rest of these out, and I'll let ya hit me again."

Ugh. He's so frustrating. I won't let him work his evil ways on me and make me laugh again. "I don't want to hit you. Well…maybe a little." I hope he hears the playfulness in my voice.

"Well, crap. That's all I have, but we're finishing anyway. Ten more."

Ready to get this over with, I push the bar up with my legs ten more times. It's not as bad as I made it sound. Yeah, I feel the burn, but for some reason, I like leg days the best. Tegan runs me through two more exercises. By the time we're done, I don't know what it is, but tears threaten to fall from my eyes. I don't ask for much. I'm not looking for miracles, but I wanted something more than one freaking pound. "I gotta go."

Weaving my way through all the machines and people I fight my tears. It's stupid. I know it, but they're standing there, begging to burst free anyway. Tegan's behind me. I'm not sure how I know it, but I do. Maybe I can somehow smell that mixture of soap and ocean he always carries or maybe I can feel his eyes on me as I waddle away, but whatever it is, I know he's there.

Before I make it too far, I feel his hand on my arm, steering me into his cubicle. "Annabel—"

I hold up my hand. If he keeps going, I'll cry. How mortifying would it be to break down in front of him? As always, Tegan's there to push me, stopping me when I try to leave again. "No, listen to me. You've kicked ass this week."

"Yeah, *one* pound of ass. Actually, not even that. Three quarters of one."

122

"And? Does that take away from everything you've done? Wipe away the hours you've spent here? The hard work? The sweat? Nope. It takes time."

I feel my resolve splitting, the anger somehow diminishing, but leaving the sadness. How does he do that? "But it sucks... I wanted... God, I don't know what I expected."

He sighs and I realize how close he's standing to me. All lean muscles, soap, ocean, and...something that always seems to make me feel better. "You expected what everyone does, which is like super results or something. It doesn't happen that way and you don't want it to happen that way. You're doing everything right here. Well, almost everything."

His words get under my skin. Not in a good or bad way, just in a Tegan way. "Oh perfect one, what am I doing wrong?" My sarcasm starts melting away the sadness now. Or maybe that's Tegan's work too.

"You want this, right? Tell me you want it."

"I want it. Hello? Isn't that why I'm here?"

He takes a step closer and I nearly pass out. That's the affect he has. "Always so sarcastic." Again, closer. Is it possible for him to get any closer? I sort of want to find out. "You want it. You're determined; those are all good, but now I need you to start believing."

"I…" I what? My mouth is opening, trying to tell him I believe I can do this, but for some reason, the words won't come out.

"I told you, I think people can do anything. I learned that from my bratty little brother. Now you need to start believing you can do it. Here," he touches my forehead and I shiver. Like seriously shiver. "And here." He touches a hand over my heart. Now, my legs go weak and it has nothing to do with the hour workout I just had. "I seriously think…I *have* to think that if you want something enough, if you find a way to make yourself believe it, it will happen. The question is, can you do that?"

I'm not sure I can do anything. Not right now, with the way his hand is on me. Embarrassingly enough, I don't even trust myself to speak so instead, I nod my head. Logically, I know he's just trying to be supportive. That part of this comes from his brother, but can't I just pretend it's all about me? That he cares, that he wants to touch me as much as my body wants to be touched?

"You gotta have faith, Annabel. And remember, you're building muscle, too. You're not always going to see a huge drop. And I hate to say this, but like you said, you haven't weighed in a while. That week off could have set you back more than you realize." His hand is still there. Mayday! His hand is still there and I don't know what to do! Couple that with my need to believe he's right. My want to really have faith that I can do this and I'm a mess right now. Up, down, backward, forward, one pound, ten. I don't know or care in this moment. It's only one little touch, but I feel it everywhere. From the tips of my toes to the top of my head, I feel him.

Dropping his hand, he steps away. "See ya next time."

As fast as my legs will carry me, without it looking like I'm running away, I do just that—run away. In the locker room, I wash up at mock speed or however that saying goes. The whole time I'm slipping on my jeans and purple button-up shirt I'm wondering what the heck is going on. He touched me. Like, in a different way than usual. Or maybe I'm imagining things, but it definitely felt different.

I slide some lip gloss over my lips, a little mascara and I'm done.

Without my direction, my eyes scan the gym for Tegan, but I don't see him. When I step outside, he's there in a pair of white shorts. They're long like guys wear them, resting mid knee, and a black t-shirt. It must have taken me longer to get ready than I thought if he's gotten off and changed in that amount of time.

Before he sees me, his mom's van pulls up in front of him. The side door opens and Tim is sitting there. A second later his mom walks around the vehicle.

"Annabel! Hi!" She waves frantically at me.

Tegan whips around, gives me a quick nod of his head and then turns back to his brother. "What's up, kid?" he playfully pushes Tim's arm. "Oh, and hi to you too Mom."

I smile at them, but have yet to get a word in.

"Dude, I'm not five. Stop calling me kid," Tim says. And when Tegan ruffles his hair, "You suck."

"Alright, stop it you two." Dana waves me over so I join them. I can't keep my eyes off them and the way they interact together. I've seen Dana and Tim, but it's even different adding Tegan to the mix.

126

"You suck," Tegan throws back at his brother like he's the one who's five. This is going to sound stupid, but if I didn't get the warm and tinglies from him before, I'm definitely getting a case of them now. No matter what, it's obvious how much he loves his brother.

"I knew Timmy had his practice and I wanted to go." He shrugs like it's not a big deal, but by the way his mom's eyes are wide, I'm pretty sure it is a big deal.

"Wow... my responsibility straddled son took extra time off? It's a miracle, but well deserved." She looks at me and then back to him.

"Drop it, Mom."

"My names, Tim. How many times do I have to tell you to call me, Tim?"

I'm getting whiplash trying to keep up with them and I love it.

And then, like she just realized she hadn't and that it's a rule she needs to, Dana gives me a quick hug. Her nails are short, unpolished and her cast is gone. Mom would never be caught dead with nails like hers.

"What time's practice, Timmy?" Tegan asks. He still hasn't acknowledged me. It makes me feel stupid for standing here.

"Tim," his brother counters.

"No, I'm Tegan. You're Timmy."

"Ha ha. So funny."

Again, they're making me dizzy with all this back and forth, but I'm smiling. It's so fun to watch.

"Focus boys. It's in ten minutes, as if you didn't know that. We're going to be late if we don't hurry."

"Okay. We can come back for my car later." Tegan gives me a quick smile. "See ya later, Annabel Lee." Then he turns like he's going to get in. Park Tegan is gone and it's distant Tegan. I don't get it. Why he's different with me around his family—unless…unless he's embarrassed of me.

"Oh!" Dana jumps like she just had the best idea in the world. "Do you want to come with us, sweetie?" She looks at me. "I know Tim would love it. This kid will look for any reason to show off. Cards, basketball."

I open my mouth to say no, but Tegan beats me to it. "I'm sure she has better things to do than tag along with us." Even though I planned to say no anyway, the fact that he did it for me hurts.

"Come on, Annabel." Tim adds. "Tegan's too grumpy."

"Am not."

"Are so." The two of them go at it again.

Finally I jump in. "Thanks a ton for asking, Tim, but I have a few errands to run. How about you keep track of how many baskets you make and tell me later? I bet you get a bunch." My voice is sad because I suddenly really want to go watch him.

Tim nods and then looks down like he's disappointed. My eyes leave him and find Tegan's which are pinned on me. It's one of those moments where I feel like he's seeing more than I'm trying to show. Maybe even more than I know.

"Screw the errands. You should come," the words rush out of his mouth like if he doesn't get them out quickly, he'll explode.

Now, I'm suffering a massive coronary. Does he want me to come or is he sacrificing something else for his brother? "I…"

Tim, Dana, they disappear behind an imaginary curtain. It's only Tegan and I standing there.

Do you really want me to come? I try to make my look say.

A half-smile curls his lips and he kind of shrugs. Not a whatever shrug, but a I'm-at-a-loss shrug. I'm not sure either of us know what we want to do or why.

"Come on. You never know, you might have fun." Tegan's still staring at me.

"I…" How many times have I started a sentence with I and never made it past the word?

"Yes," he says.

"Yes," I confirm. What in the world is going on here?

Chapter Ten

164.9 TOTALLY HANGING OUT WITH TEGAN'S FAMILY

We all climb out of Dana's van, Tegan going straight for the back to get the wheelchair. I'm a big ball of nerves as I step out of the car, still shocked that I'm even here with him. After he pulls the chair out, Tegan tries to help Timmy get out, but he pushes his hand away.

"I can do it."

"I know." Tegan steps back, holding the chair and letting his brother pull himself into it. It's amazing to watch him. How well he can get around. His mom reaches in and pulls out a basketball before closing up. It's an old, rundown basketball court on the same side of town as the gym. Metal bleachers are next to it. There are other people in wheelchairs already on the court. Tegan holds out his hand, and Dana passes him the ball. He dribbles over to the court with Tim, as we walk to the bleachers.

A minute later, Tegan's passing Tim the ball and joining us.

I can't take my eyes off them. They're all teenagers except for the coach who is in a wheelchair himself. They're not playing a game or anything, but running drills like they would at any other basketball game: shooting, passing, stuff like that.

"Pretty cool, huh?" I'm in the middle of Tegan and his mom, but I notice him much more.

"Yeah. It's incredible."

"They haven't played games or anything yet. Ed, the coach, he does this on his own. It's not a real league or anything, but he's working on it, trying to find people for them to play.

I'm in awe. How did I not know this went on? I can't take my eyes off Tim and the guys, passing the ball around and shooting. They're good. Better than I could ever hope to be. "I think this is probably the coolest thing I've ever seen." I'm envious. That they're out there, no fear, and going for it. I could never do that. It's inspiring.

I manage to tear my eyes from the court to look at Tegan. He's studying me so intensely that I know he's discovered something. Some deep, dark secret to me that I never knew was there.

"We can thank Tegan for finding it for him. We never would have known about it otherwise." Dana smiles at her son.

"You found this for Tim?" My insides turn into mush. Not the blubbery kind either. This is dangerous territory, but I'm feeling like a rebel. "That's...sweet."

He doesn't reply, only turns to look at his brother again so I do the same. We don't talk any more. Their practice only lasts about forty-five minutes and afterward everyone else packs up and takes off except for Tim. He waves his brother over.

"I'll be right back."

He traipses down the bleachers. A minute later he's dribbling the ball around his brother. You can see the concentration on Tim's face, waiting for the perfect time. Then he strikes, stealing the ball from Tegan. He doesn't dribble it, but holds it on his lap as he wheels toward the basket and shoots.

"Lucky shot!" Tegan harasses him.

It's awesome to watch. He's awesome. I can't help but say it. "He's amazing."

It takes a minute before I realize I just called him amazing in front of his mom. She doesn't flinch, tease or anything. She only smiles, lost in her boys the way I just got lost in Tegan. Well…maybe not the *exact* same way.

"He is, isn't he?" She sounds almost sad. "He tries to do everything. Thinks he can hold up the whole world. He's so smart, funny. God he used to love life. A little troublemaker, but nothing bad. Now he's like a fifty-year-old guy trapped in an eighteen-year-old body. Works like crazy. Even when he was still in high school. Always packing money away for college, to help me, even though I won't take it. Goes to every appointment of Tim's that he can. I think he thinks he can try and give his brother back everything we lost."

The wall is completely down now. Any doubts I had about him, vanished, eaten up by his mom's words. He's more than amazing. Part of me hopes my silence will fuel her to fill it. To give me more information on him, but then I feel guilty. I want whatever I know about Tegan to come from him.

Tim saves me. "Annabel. Come down and play. Tegan's already wussing out on me!"

"Yeah right! I don't even know how to dribble a basketball!" I call back, but stand anyway. Then I remember Dana was talking, but when I glance back, she's waving me toward them. Tim tosses me the ball when I get to them.

"Everyone can dribble. Just do it and see if I can get it from you."

Tegan steps back, smirking at me, but I ignore him. This is for Tim. I start to bounce the ball and he wheels toward me. When he gets close enough, I pick it up to turn around.

"Hey! That's cheating!"

"It is? Crap, sorry."

"Yeah, you can't move your feet with the ball in your hand. It's traveling."

I dribble again, concentrating on what I'm doing. Tim comes toward me again and I slowly jog away, still dribbling the ball. It doesn't bounce off my foot or anything. "Hey! I'm pretty good at this," I laugh, but then he pokes his hand out and the ball slips away from me.

Maybe not…

"Okay, wait. I'm trying that again." Determined this time, I dribble again. I head down the court, not too fast, but Tim is right next to me. When I get to the basket, I stop, unsure of what to do."

"You're supposed to shoot!" Tim is so close now and duh. How could I have not thought of that? I toss the ball up and hit bounces off the rim. Hard and flies right back at me. I duck because balls flying at my head is so not my thing.

Tim busts up laughing. I can't help it. I start too. I'm grabbing my stomach for cracking up so much. "Oh my God. I suck."

"Totally," Tim agrees.

"Hey! You're not supposed to agree with me." I playfully push his arm.

Tim yells toward his brother, "Did you see how bad she sucks, Teag?"

Tegan! I forgot he was there. He and his mom are standing outside the court watching us. Dana is smiling. Tegan's eyes burn into me. Automatically I take a step back, thinking I did something wrong, but then he shifts and I see something else.

Thanks. His look seems to say.

My pleasure. And it was.

***

It's not often I watch TV downstairs. Well, it's not really often I watch TV at all, but that's beside the point. Em's with her mom and I don't feel like being cooped up in my room so I'm sitting downstairs using the TV for background noise while really, I'm mentally dissecting my life.

No matter how many ways or times I run it over in my head, I still can't believe I hung out with Tegan and his family. I'm looking for a reason, in it. I need a reason for it, but I can't find one. Besides the obvious that they asked I mean. But why?

And Tegan. At first it seemed like he didn't want me to go, but then he asked. I'm not an idiot. I'm pretty sure that only happened because it's Tegan's way of giving his brother what he wanted, but still.

He asked.

And then he watched me. Watched me in a way he never had before. Unfortunately, I'm not as good at dissecting boys as I am myself so I have no clue what his look meant, but *God,* I want it to mean something good.

My cell chirps, making me jump. It's a text from Tegan. I know because I totally saved his number the last time he texted me.

Hey, Annabel Lee. What ya up 2?

I giggle. *Giggle* over a stupid, freaking text. **Not much. Just hanging out. You?**

On a break at work. Listen, just wanted to say thx for hanging out. For playin with Timmy. That was cool.

Some of the air seeps out of my balloon. Of course he only wanted to talk because of his brother.

No problem. Had fun. Tim's awesome.

Don't tell him that.

I don't text again, because I'm not sure how to reply. There's not really much else to say.

You still there? Tegan texts a couple minutes later.

Yeah.

Gotta head back to work. Just wanted to say hi and... See you soon, Annabel Lee.

No matter what his reason for texting, I still can't help but smile. **See you soon.**

Behind me, the front door slams. I turn to see Mom walk in. She heads straight to the kitchen. Maybe I'm a glutton for punishment. Maybe I just want to talk to her. I'm not sure the reason, but I get up and follow her. "Hi. You're home early."

"I have some work to do, but all my notes are here. What are you doing?"

I shrug. "Not much. Did you get a new client or something?"

———

138

"No. It's pageant stuff."

Pageant stuff. Again, glutton for punishment? Riding a high from Tegan's text? Whatever it is, it forces a lie to come out of my mouth. "I had fun helping the other day... The pageant thing... it might be kind of fun."

No, hell hasn't frozen over and I don't want to participate, but I want her to offer. I want it so bad that I would probably actually say yes if she did.

Mom shakes her head. "Oh, come on Annabel. You don't have to pretend you like it. I know better."

I know better too. I shouldn't have even brought it up.

Chapter Eleven

CHA-CHA-CHANGES

It's an hour before I'm supposed to meet Tegan at the gym for our workout when I get a text. I'll never get used to seeing his name pop up on my screen. It's so crazy, the thought that he's texted me a few times lately.

Bad news. Had something to take care of. Had to get someone to cover my shift. You're working out with Brian today.

No. No, no, no, no. I don't like this. Not at all. I'm totally a creature of habit. I'm used to working out with Tegan and I don't want to work out with anyone else.

Maybe I can reschedule?

What? No. It's not a big deal. Brian's cool. You'll be fine. Gotta go.

I'll be fine? That just shows how little he knows about me. Not that he really should know anything about me, but still. My stomach is already upset at the thought of working out with someone else.

My phone beeps one more time.

We'll jog tonight too, k? Really going now.

I take a couple deep breaths. I can do this. I'm going to do this. What's the big deal, right? My jog tonight with Tegan will be my reward, if I can make it through my hour with Brian. Still, I wish he would have at least gotten me a girl.

There's no one waiting for me by the door when I get there. The girl at the front desk tells me where to find Brian. When I do, he's playing on his phone.

"Hi. I'm Annabel. Tegan said to meet you today?"

He's probably mid-twenties. A nice smile, but it still feels weird. Yes, I know I'm a dork. This shouldn't be as big a deal as it is.

"Hi. Nice to meet you." He holds out his hand and I shake it.

Brian leads me upstairs and I do my cardio. Alone. Twenty minutes later he comes up to get me and then we go into my work out. He's nice and all. Answers my questions. Gives me direction, but it's not the same. He doesn't cheer me on the same way. Doesn't interact. Well, unless you count with his phone.

I'm not sure I could have stuck with this if Brian was my trainer. With him I feel like what I am—just a client, not a person. It makes me so thankful for what I have. Somehow, even though I know Tegan doesn't jog with everyone, I know he doesn't treat them the way Brian does.

"Five more," Brian tells me.

"I can't..." The words make me mad. I should be able to do this. I have done it, but right now, I just don't feel like I can.

"Just try."

Not, you can do it. Try. It shouldn't matter. The logical part of me knows I shouldn't need that—I should be able to do it on my own.

I let the weights clank down. I'm done.

***

It's strange meeting Tegan tonight for some reason. Maybe it's because it's the first time we've met in the evening or because it's the first time I've worked out and gone jogging in the same day. Or maybe it's because it felt so weird to work out with someone who wasn't him. Whatever the reason is, I almost feel like this is the first time we've hung out. It's more than just butterflies in my belly: fireflies and lightening bugs join the swarm.

This time we meet at the park. It's slightly busier in the evening than the morning, but still not overwhelmingly so. He's in basketball shorts like he always wears when we jog and a Celtic jersey. I know enough to know there aren't many Celtics fans in California.

"Hey you," he says when I get out of the car. Ever since our day at the court with his family, he's been light like this. More open. It makes me all warm and gooey inside. Dangerous for my heart, but true.

"Hey."

We stretch a little and then fall into our familiar jog.

"How'd your work out go today, Annabel Lee?" It still gets to me how he's never breathless when we run. I'm not an idiot. I know he could go much faster than he does with me, but still I wish it affected him a little more than it does.

"Okay, I guess." I fight to keep my voice steady. Thinking about Mom and how much I disappoint her. Then working out with someone else at the gym. It hasn't been the best day.

"Just okay? Did ya miss me?" he laughs like it's a joke, but I did. I missed him. When I don't reply he speaks again. "I'd have much rather been there, too. It was a court thing we had to go to...don't really feel like talking about it though."

———

143

As much as I want to know, I'm thankful for what he gave me. We jog in silence a little longer. No noise but the sound of steps mixing together again. "So... is something else up? You're quiet tonight."

I want to talk about it. It's unreal how badly. It's different talking to Em who knows Mom and will just blast her. Or Dad who will come up with a way to defend her while still trying to build me up too. Running? Somehow it helps. Maybe because I won't have to look at him. I concentrate on my steps, my breathing. "It's my mom. We got into it today. She just... I'm not who she wants. As a daughter I mean. She wants perfect and I'm not that." Exhale breath. I can't believe I did it.

"No one is perfect, Annabel Lee."

"She is."

"Nope. Maybe she's just better at hiding it. There's nothing wrong with who you are and it sucks she makes you think there is."

"Yeah it does suck. Can I ask you something?" My words come out much choppier than they should.

"You wanna know how Timmy got hurt."

I don't reply because I don't have to.

144

"Freak sporting accident. Can you believe that shit? Who expects that? For an eleven year old boy who looks up to his brother, to head out of the house with a football under his arm and end up in the hospital because he'll never walk again?"

Football… Oh, God. And was Tegan playing with him?

It's on the tip of my tongue to apologize, but I don't. Somehow, I know he wouldn't want it. "Sucks."

"Sure as hell does." He picks up speed. "Come on. I'll race you the final stretch."

"You cheat!" I call after him as I push my legs harder, faster. Of course I don't beat him, but I don't end up too far behind so for me, it's a win. I'm gasping for breath as he's handing me a water bottle. I suck half the thing down. "You totally didn't win."

"Yeah, I totally did." He mocks.

Feigning anger I cross my arms a little too hard. It squeezes my water bottle which then squirts water at my face.

Holy. Freaking. Embarrassing.

Laugher bursts out of Tegan's mouth. I want to be mad, but I can't. I start laughing too. "AHHH. I hate you!" I point my bottle at him and squeeze. He doesn't move as the rest of my water sprays at him. He's too busy laughing. Our giggling mingles together the way our footsteps did not along ago.

When we finally stop, we're both breathing hard. Standing close. In this moment, I know my life is about to change.

"Go out with me," Rushes out of his mouth so quickly, I'm not sure I heard him right.

"Huh?" *Please, God. Don't let me have been hearing things. Don't let me die of shock before I can say yes. No! I mean before I get to go.*

"Go out with me. This weekend." I'm sure I look like one of those wrinkle dogs with the really big eyes, because they're wide and staring and I can't help it. "Like a date."

"A date?"

"A date." Snicker. "I can't seem to get enough of you."

"Why?" Is it the coolest question to ask in this situation? Nope, but it's what I need to know.

"Say yes." He's smirking.

There was never a chance at me answering any differently. "Yes."

"I'll text you. We'll see each other before that, but I'll text you anyway."

I can't stop smiling.

Chapter Twelve

TWO DATES—HOLY CRAP!

Tegan texts me a few times as the week goes on. Nothing major, but then that's what makes them special.

What ya up to?

I think my family likes you more than me.

Are you excited for this weekend?

We're still on our same workout schedule and when we're there, we only talk "business". Basically, that just means he wants to drive me crazy. Which he's doing. The one time I brought it up, I asked him what I should wear and he said, "Just be yourself. Wear whatever you feel comfortable in." What does that even mean? I can wear my jammies, because that's what I feel comfortable in.

But I can't do that. In fact, I'm so desperate, I'm heading to Mom's office to talk to her. Not to tell her I'm going on a date, obviously, but the fact is, I need her help. Which totally kills me, knowing what she thinks of me. Knowing that even though she will *want* to make me over, she'll also still not be happy with the outcome.

It's only 8:00 and she's already perfectly put together.

"Mom?"

"Yeah." She doesn't look up from her computer. It's been like this since our talk about the pageant. Short, one word answers. Things are more strained between us than they have ever been.

My words want to stick in my mouth like a huge wad of gum, but I find a way to speak around it. "I thought maybe we could do the spa day today. Maybe get my hair and my nails done like you said. I have to meet Em this afternoon, so we'd have to be back, but—"

"Perfect!" She cuts me off. "Go get changed and I'll call and make our appointment!"

An hour later we're sitting with our feet in a tub of water. They've been scrubbed, but oh, here they go, scrubbing them again. Our nails are painted, then I'm subjected to the same thing to my hands: clip, massage, paint. I hate to admit it kind of feels good. Who doesn't like to be pampered? At the same time, it feels weird because it's not me.

"What do you think you want to do with your hair?" Mom asks, eyes closed and head back while she enjoys the pampering.

"Well—"

"Oh, I know! I'm thinking bangs, layers around your face and some honey colored highlights. You don't want blond with your dark hair. That screams trashy." Why did she ask me if she didn't even plan to hear my answer?

What did I get myself into? I'm really not feeling the whole layer thing. I like how my hair is now. All one length, no bangs, and resting on my shoulders. Layers only mean I'm going to have to do something with it every day, but instead of saying that, I agree with her. "Sure. Whatever you think."

"You'll love it, Annabel. It's amazing what hair and nails can do for you. Even the plainest women have options nowadays."

That stings. Is that me? Am I the plain girl she's talking about? I know the answer to that question. Tegan likes my eyes and so do I. They match hers. I wonder if she's ever even noticed. "Cool."

After our nails are done, it's onto the hair. I watch as short black strands fall to the ground, both hopeful and irritated at the same time. Why didn't I speak up if I don't want my hair layered? But...what if it looks good? I shouldn't shoot down "options" before I test them out, right?

Mom's giddy as they dye and cut my hair. Me? I'm not really sure how I feel. I'm faced away from the mirrors on Mom's suggestion, not seeing makes it worse on my already overactive nerves.

"All done!" They turn me around and I freeze. It doesn't look bad. Actually, it looks kind of good. It just doesn't look like me.

"What do you think? Isn't it gorgeous, Annabel?"

"Yeah...gorgeous. Are you sure?"

"Of course I'm sure. Aren't you sure?"

"Yes, I'm sure." But I'm not. I'm not sure at all. I feel strange... different. That's normal, I think. Anytime you do something different, it must feel like this.

Then I think of Tegan. I know it's stupid, but what's he going to think? Am I trying too hard? Is he going to see right through it? Ugh. I hate this! But I don't have much time to contemplate it. A minute later Mom is dragging me out the door and clothes shopping.

"Mom, dresses really aren't my thing." I try to tell her as she looks through the rack.

"Not all dresses, no. But there are some that work wonders, Annabel. If it's styled right, it brings out your...assets and hides the...imperfections."

My heart drops. I didn't mean they don't look good on me. I meant I don't like them.

"This whole shop is for women like you. I promise, you'll be so happy when we're done." She touches my cheek. It's the first time she's touched me like this in forever. "You'll be pretty."

I'll be pretty. Because I'm not now. I try to smile. "Thanks, Mom. You're the best."

And then we finish our mother/daughter day. I think it's the only one we've ever had that she's enjoyed.

***

On my way to the gym to meet Tegan, I change. I already feel like my insides are going to explode from nerves that I have to at least be comfortable in my clothes. I can't do much about the hair, but the clothes are going.

Off goes the skirt for a pair of khaki capris. I cover up the tank top with a button up shirt that reaches my elbows. I feel like I'm jacked up on some kind of upper drug I've never taken. Make sense? Okay, I know it doesn't, but I can't explain it any other way. I'm twitchy, on edge as excitement and nerves fight to see which one will take me over.

The second I kill the engine in my BMW and look up, I feel like I'm going to puke. Tegan stands there waiting for me and he's gorgeous. More gorgeous than any other time I've seen him, if that's possible. Like always, he's wearing shorts. These are black, hanging mid-knee like they always do. White socks, black and white Nikes, a white t-shirt with button up shirt over his too, though I'm sure his is more for hotness reasons rather than fear of arm flab.

His slightly wavy hair is wet, like he got out of the shower right before coming. In his hand is a smoothie cup, which makes me want to laugh, but I can't because I can't get over how good he looks. His eyes are on me, and those masculine plump lips are stretched into a smile. The jerk. He knows I'm looking and I immediately cast my eyes down. My foot itches to push down on the accelerator, to run while my heart is fully intact, before I fall too much, but I don't. I'm tired of missing out and if he wants me here, even just for this one date, I'm staying. I deserve this.

I get out of the car and step onto the sidewalk in front of him. The pulse in my ears drowns out the traffic speeding down the street. Yeah, I'm so gone. "Hey."

He doesn't reply for a minute, reaching out and fingering my hair. The strands slip through his fingers and brush my cheek. It's almost like he's touching me and I shiver. "What did you do, Annabel Lee?"

Embarrassment weakens my determination from a few seconds ago. I wring my hands together. "Color my hair? You know it's when—" Tegan cuts off my attempt at sarcasm.

"I know what you did, smart-aleck. It looks nice, it's just. I don't know, different. I'm not complaining. You look pretty, I just want to be sure you did this because it's something you want, not because of our date or something."

"You're such a flirt. Quit calling me pretty," is what comes out of my mouth when what I really want to say is, can you please repeat that? Like ten times. Thanks.

"You do that a lot, deflect compliments like that. I mean, if you wanted to call me pretty, I'd be glad to hear it. Okay, maybe not pretty, but sexy. You want to call me sexy, don't you? Admit it." He's got that mischievous smile on his face and I'm at a loss for words. He always finds a way to steal them from me. Which I think is the point. I try and deflect compliments and I think he's trying to deflect my nerves. I melt a little more inside.

"Seriously though. It's pretty, but I liked it before too."

Thump. Thump. Thump. It's hard to think over the sound of my heart. "Thanks. It was my mom's idea. She likes playing makeover Barbie with me. I finally let her."

"Hmm." He crosses his arms. "Next time, tell her you're fine the way you are." Then he grabs my hand, twining our fingers together in a way that shoots sparks up my arm and down my chest. "Come on, we're burning daylight. I'm ready to have some fun. I need it today."

It makes me think something happened, but I don't ask. If he wants to tell me, he will.

Once he closes the passenger door for me, I do a little giddy dance inside. There's nothing wrong with being an independent woman, but there's also nothing wrong with a guy going the extra mile. Not that I have a lot of experience in the situation, but I digress. Once he closes my door and gets in, Tegan turns to me. "So, I was thinking the fair because...well, because I'm obsessed with rides, but then my know-it-all mom brought up the fact that I don't know if you do rides or not. I told her all I had to do is challenge you and you'd do it, but then I figured that might not be the best thing for our first date."

I love this side of him so much. Love how he's so much more relaxed around me lately. And somehow, I'm the same around him. "Hey! What is that supposed to mean?"

155

"Nothing bad. Just that you're determined. If you think someone doesn't believe you can do something, you're going to."

"And how do you know that?"

He raises his eyebrows. "Because I'm good?"

And cocky. "Try again."

"Because that's how I get you to do what I want at the gym."

"Whatever."

"We're getting off track here. My second thought was the zoo because, well... nobody goes to the zoo anymore."

The unease in my belly has started to lift and I'm falling deeper into the comfort that Tegan brings. Plus, could he have picked cooler things to do for our date? "Well, we're in trouble because I can't choose. I love the fair and I haven't been to the zoo in years. Both would be good."

"Well, it's," he picks up his cell and glances at it. "Wow, just now three. You were early."

"Not as early as you."

For the first time, I get a bashful look from him before his eyes return to the road. "Okay, so we can do both? What do you think? Hit the zoo. Leave about six, get to the fair about six thirty. What time do you have to be home?"

"Midnight." Mom thinks I'm out to dinner and a movie with Em tonight. She never calls Em's house and Em always uses my cell to call me so I there's no way I'll get caught by either of them. Man, what a liar I am turning out to be.

"That works then. You game, Annabel Lee?"

"Sounds perfect!" Perfect? What the frig? Maybe I should just throw myself at him while I'm at it? Luckily Tegan doesn't comment on it, giving me the chance to A) Change the subject and B) Ask him something I've wanted to for a while now.

"So...what's with the name? Rocky I get, but Annabel Lee?"

"Don't tell me... No, it can't be true."

My heart does the nervous, skip-a-beat-thing. Is this something I'm supposed to know? I have a feeling I just missed an obvious answer on the 'cool teen test'. "Just tell me."

"It's Poe. You know, the poet? Don't tell me you've never read *Annabel Lee*?"

Aww, he's kind of nerdy and I didn't know it. It makes me like him all the more, not that I need a reason to.

Tegan rubs a hand over his head and cocks his head to look at me from the side. No. I definitely don't need another reason to like this boy. His looks are reason enough. "No. Of course I know who Poe is, but never read the poem. My best friend Emily is obsessed with him. I'm sure she knows it."

"Emily has good taste."

Jealousy creeps up on me like a monster in a scary movie. "I have good taste, too." Once the words are out, I realize I sound like such a spoiled brat looking for attention. What does he do to me?

Tegan reaches over and squeezes my leg. Yes! He squeezes my leg and I'm too distracted by the pulsing energy zipping from him to me to even wonder if I feel flabby. It's an innocent touch, but my hormones, they don't want to see it that way. It's embarrassing to admit, but I feel faint.

"Well obviously. You're out with me, right?" Before I can tell him how conceited he is, he speaks again. "Kidding. But yeah, I don't doubt your taste."

"Um, thanks…" His car suddenly feels hot. Like stifling hot. I hit the button to let the window down a little bit, hoping the fresh air can do something to cool me off, because if not, I just might combust from this Near Tegan Experience.

"I loved English in high school. Did I ever tell you that?" He says as he drives off.

"No." I want to hear about it now. I want to know everything.

"Yep. Used to be what I wanted to go to college for. You know…before."

My heart kind of breaks for him. I don't get it. If he loves English, it's what he should do.

We talk a little more on the way to the zoo. Not about anything important: the gym, college. He's staying local and will only be forty-five minutes away in the fall. I don't say anything, but I'm planning on attending Berkley as well and not because of him either.

When we get to the zoo, I pull out money to pay for myself.

"What are you doing?" Tegan asks.

"You shouldn't have to pay." Add this to the list of stupid things I've said. Yes, I know the guy usually pays on a date and I'm not one of those girls who gets her panties in a wad if the guy wants to be a gentleman, but I also didn't want to make any assumptions. As far as I know, this is a friend thing. Maybe Tegan's in the market for a new BFF or something and I don't want to look like the love-struck girl who assumes we're on a date/date.

He hands the attendant the money and gets our tickets before replying. Once we're away from her prying ears he says. "I don't know what kind of dates you've been on, but they must have been douches if they made you pay. I'm taking *you* out, Annabel Lee."

When Tegan threads his fingers through mine, I do a giddy jig inside which breaks into a full on Disney movie song and dance segment, complete with talking birds and little mice friends. And I know it's dumb. I know I'll probably get hurt. There's a huge possibility this won't end well, but I don't care. It feels too good. *He* feels too good and from now on, that's all I'm going to concentrate on.

"So, what do you want to look at first? Lions, Tigers, Elephants? We have the whole zoo at our fingertips."

But it doesn't feel like just the zoo. This very second, for the first time, it feels like I have the world at my fingertips and I'm going to reach out and grab it. Even if it's only temporary. Or if he only seems to like me because his family does, I'm taking it.

***

We start out at the monkeys. I've never been particularly fond of monkeys or anything, but it's what we happen upon first. From there we go to apes, birds, snakes. Our hands are never apart as we walk around, taking in the animals in their manmade habitats. And it's fun. Tegan laughs when the monkeys wrestle around with each other, joking about me giving them fighting lessons. His laughter is contagious and I can't help but catch it. Not that I want to help it.

We look at elephants and I almost freak out when we see the llamas. They drool like crazy and I swear I start to gag. With more of that infectious laughter, Tegan pulls me away. I cover my eyes with my hands. "Ugh! That is the grossest thing I've ever seen. I have such a weak gag reflex."

"You're such a wuss." His hand pulls from mine and before I can miss it, he wraps an arm around me, pulling me to his chest so I can bury my face in it. And I do. Boy do I ever.

"I'll save you from attack of the killer drool. Come on, stay close and it won't get you."

His voice is deeper, huskier and I stumble a little, our feet tangling. Instead of embarrassment that I almost trip us, I giggle.

"Shh, this is no time for laughing. We're in serious trouble here. Just keep close and I'll get us out of this."

"Are you sure you can handle it?" I tease him, getting into the game he's playing because it gets me closer to him. When I'm like this, he's all I feel: warmth and long muscles. He's all I smell: soap and ocean. I'm not his client or the outcast at school. I'm just a girl with a boy.

"Of course I can. I handle everything. Like I said, you might want to stay close though. You never know when drool wielding llamas will jump out at you. I'll protect you."

We're walking and I don't care where we're going. My eyes are no longer in his chest, so I can see, but I'm closer to him than I've ever been to any boy. "I thought I was the one with the nice hook though?"

"Baby…you ain't seen moves until you've seen mine." The words are spoken with that signature playfulness Tegan uses. It's so easy for boys to say things like that, nonchalantly like it doesn't mean anything. But for me, the word *baby* nuzzles its way into all the most important parts of me. For me it means everything.

"I…I think we're safe now." Slowly, I pull away. I want to kick my own butt for the separation, but widen it at the same time. Man, Tegan is right. I'm a girl, but I still confuse myself.

"There you go, ruining my fun. I was planning on kicking some serious llama ass, you know."

162

I don't reply, keeping my eyes forward until we reach the panda bears.

"Oh! Let's stop here. I want to look."

"Of course you do. Pandas are such a girl thing."

My eyes roll. "And that's such a boy thing to say."

We're the only ones at the Panda exhibit. It's tucked into a little corner making it feel like there's no one in the world but me, Tegan and the two bears I see behind the glass. The white on their fur is all dirty, but they're still pretty.

"Sounds stupid, but they look so sweet. It's like I could go in there and cuddle up with one."

"Dangerous. You thought drool was deadly."

"They don't look it though. I mean, I know they are, but… let's just say I get why people sleep with teddy bears at night. It's like that's what they're meant for." I hear the wind rustle through the trees around us. It's almost like our day at the park and then I feel him, Tegan's right behind me, his front against my back. The soap and ocean is all I know right now. This boy totally turns me into one of those swooning, love obsessed girls I used to make fun of. Right now, I'm swooning on the inside.

"Look." He's closer. Touching me, his breath a whisper in my hair, against my ear.

"Where?" My heart is going crazy. My voice all husky like I'm some seductress or something. It's kind of cool, and I'm not even doing it on purpose. I couldn't control my voice if I wanted to right now.

Tegan points and I try with everything in me to follow his finger, but all I can focus on is him. Surrounding me. Blanketing me.

"Over there. See in the back corner. It's a baby. If the mama wasn't in there, you could cuddle with that one."

Really, I just want to cuddle with him. He's going straight to my head. I suck in a breath. *Oh my God, oh my God, oh my God.* I don't know what to do or say right now. Do I move? Let him stand here all night if he wants to? I turn around. It's even harder this way because his face is so close. So very close I can see a small chip in one of his teeth. Minty toothpaste mingles with his scent.

I bite my lips when he pushes a strand of hair behind my ear. He's smiling. I'm dying of shock over here and he's smiling, but yeah, it's a nice smile. Knowing or not, I can't help but admire it.

Tegan leans closer to me. "Annabel Lee..."

"What?" Even to me, my voice sounds far off.

Closer…he's closer. He's going to kiss me. I'm caught between wanting to scream hallelujah and having a heart attack.

"What are we going to do with you?" I have no idea what his words mean, but I know what I want him to do with me. I want his lips on mine.

"I…I don't know."

And then his hand drops.

He steps away.

I want nothing more than to pull him back to me.

"We should keep going. Not much more time before we have to leave."

I can't help but feel rejected.

Chapter Thirteen

PRIZES, RIDES, AND KISSES, OH MY!

"Okay, from what I hear, it's bad date etiquette if I don't feed you. What sounds good?"

We're in the car, on our way to the fair. I'm a little hungry, but not much. Mostly, I'm just excited to get to the fair. Like I told him, I really do love rides and the games and the thought of playing them with Tegan, even if he did just leave me hanging, let's just call it an extra bonus. "Um, it's up to you. I'm not really all that hungry. I swear I won't dock you date points."

"How about something quick? We can run through a drive thru or something." What am I thinking? It's not as though McDonalds is on my diet. For some reason, it will hurt if he brings it up right now. Make all this seem like it's not really the kind of date I'm hoping it is.

"If you're cool with that, I am. We can eat in the car real quick and then head over."

We go through McDonalds. I get a salad and Tegan gets a burger. "Tell me about Emily?" he asks while we're eating in his car. His question surprises me, but also warms me. It's time I realize this guy might really want to know me. I want to know everything about him too.

"She's great. We've been best friends since we were little. We're both," Ugh, I don't want to talk about this part. "Let's just say neither of us would be starring in a teen movie unless we're the ones getting shoved into lockers." Sure, that's kind of making it sound worse than it is, but that's how it feels sometimes.

"I hate high school. It's shitty. Most people there are shitty, trying to be on top because they know it's the only time in their life they will be. I'm glad to be out of it."

If at all possible, my heart softens toward him even more. One look at Tegan and you know he would be the kind of guy who would date cheerleaders and be friends with Billy Mason, but I also know Tegan would never treat people the way Billy does. He'd never sit back and let it happen like Billy's friends either.

Before I can talk myself out of it, I look over at him and smile. "You're a good guy. I mean, nice. That's nice…You're nice."

Something in the way he looks at me changes. A little glow to his deep, woodsy eyes. Like a bonfire, the dark wood crackling with light. But then he shakes it off, throwing water on the fire. Somehow, I know he knows I'm not ready for whatever that look meant. "That just might be the best compliment I've ever gotten. You're not so bad yourself, Annabel Lee." He takes my trash from me, gets out of the car and throws it away before we're on our way to the fair.

***

"I bet I can make more baskets than you." Tegan hands the man at the basketball stand some cash.

"You only say that because you saw my awesome basketball skills with your brother. Are you supposed to be offering to win me something instead of challenging me?"

"Nope. I'm all for equal rights between girls and guys. This, baby, is a challenge. But just to spice things up a little, if you win, you have to give me your prize and if I win, I'll give you mine."

Baby… It just might be my new favorite word. "Equal opportunity my butt. You just said you knew you could win. You're trying to win me something on the sly. What if I want to win something for you?"

Tegan winks. "Then you'll have to beat me."

Of course I don't. We play twice and he wins both times, giving me two little stuffed animals. I'm not sure I've ever laughed so much in my life. We play almost every game here. Multiple times, I offer to pay. He's blowing way too much money on this date, especially when, from what his mom said, he's been trying to save it. Every time he waves me off and tell me I will get it next time, but he also said he's taking me to dinner next, too. He was right. He does always get his way.

After we do the game thing for a while, we hit up some rides. In between each one, Tegan holds my hand and I'm starting to get used to the feel of my smaller one wound up with his. It's like we've been doing this much longer than just one day.

Evening comes and goes, night settling in, little twinkles of light dotting the sky. The night is ending too fast.

"We have time for one more. I'm going to be cheesy with this one, but Ferris Wheel?" he asks.

"It's my favorite." Hand and hand, we walk over to it. As we're in line I freeze. No. No, no, no. Billy Mason is standing on the other side of the ride. Patrick and crew, along with all their girlfriends. Just seeing them threatens to magically erase the fun of the night. What if they see us? What if they say something in front of Tegan? I think I'd die.

"What's wrong?"

I shake my head.

"Come on. You know I won't let it go until you tell me."

He won't and I want to end this part of the conversation as quickly as I can. "The kings and queens of Hillcrest High. I just...I don't want to see them."

Like always, he knows the perfect thing to say. "Fuck 'em. They look like idiots anyway."

He's right. Billy keeps trying to grab Queen Cheerleader's butt. Patrick is watching his moves and trying to photo copy them with someone else. They're stumbling around like a bunch of losers. Somehow, our hands have come unlatched, but this time, it's me who grabs his. "Come on. We're next."

Once we're taking the rounds on the Ferris Wheel, I completely forget about anything but Tegan and this night. His arm is around me. *Me,* as we go round and round, taking in the sites of the fair and all the people below. Running the risk of sounding like a total girlie-girl, it's perfect.

"My parents used to love the fair. They brought us a lot when we were younger."

His words surprise me. It's the first time he's brought up more than his mom or Tim. "Can I ask, where he is? If you don't want to answer, that's okay." I hope my words don't ruin our night. We've tried to steer clear of the bad stuff.

"Typical thing." His grip on me tightens. "Didn't want to deal with his responsibilities so he left."

So many pieces of Tegan start to fall into place. Why he's so fiercely loyal and protective of his family. He won't let them get hurt again, even if that means doing everything he can for them rather than himself.

But no apologies. "Sucks."

He gives me another squeeze. This one seems to say, thank you.

Too soon it's over and we're getting out of the ride. I don't even know if Billy and his gang are still here because I don't take the time to look. The fairgrounds are emptying out, the rides closing down and we're walking hand in hand to his car.

When we get there, I try to open the passenger door, but Tegan stops me. It's a replay of our moment by the bears.

My hands are shaking as Tegan steps so very close to me. I'm probably the only almost-eighteen-year-old girl in the world who has never kissed a boy. I wonder will I be different. After the next minute, if my life will shift from before kiss to after kiss.

His hand is in my hair again, but this time, he's not just putting it behind my ear. He's threading his fingers through it like he does with our hands. His palm's buried deep, resting on the back of my neck.

Yes, I think this kiss will definitely make my life different.

Even though it's dark there's a streetlight making it so I can see him. Who the heck knows what else is around us, cars, people, an atomic bomb. All I know is us.

"I like you, Annabel Lee." I'm boxed in between Tegan and his car. His chest touches me.

"Why?" I ask.

"Because you're pretty…funny…smart…sarcastic... and you get it. Get me. Get my family."

I don't even doubt his words. How can I doubt anything he says?

"Can I tell you a secret?" he asks.

I nod.

"I knew there was something different about you from the beginning. Even if I didn't come out there to get you that first day, you would have made it in. I admire that, ya know? That you won't let anything get you down. That you keep pushing through. Just like me."

I want to tell him it's a lie. That I'm not strong at all and I'm scared to death to fail, but it feels good to have him believe in me. For him to see something in me no one else does. And again, how can I not believe his words? The way he speaks them, how they tickle my skin and seep inside, fuels me. I *am* determined and I can do anything.

I can't help it, I lick my lips.

Tegan's face is slowly, way too slowly coming toward mine. "This time, I'm really going to kiss you so if you don't want me to, you better stop me now."

"Stop? You must be crazy."

"That's even better than your last compliment."

Oh my God. Did I say that out loud? And then it doesn't matter because his lips are on mine. They're just as soft as they look, but strong too. Or maybe the kiss is just strong, eager, because it's all I feel or know. It's like I'm drowning in him.

When his tongue comes out and teases the seam of my lips, I'm done for. Sunken like a ship to the bottom of the ocean. It's weird how I know what to do, like I've done this so many times before. My mouth opens, our tongues meeting, first tentatively and then with the eager need again. I taste the mint. Smell the soap and ocean. Shiver when the hand in my hair pulls me closer to him.

In and out. Give and take, our tongues do a dance that's foreign and familiar at the same time. When his other hand touches my waist, my arms wrap around his neck. I want him closer. Closer than anyone has ever been to me. And he is, but then after one, two gentle, tongueless kisses on my lips, he's pulling away.

Tegan's forehead drops forward so it's resting against mine. "Why did that take us so long?"

***

It's been a few days since our first kiss. I say first because …we've done it a lot since then. I'm always awkward and nervous, but the second his lips touch mine, everything else melts away. And I was right. There is definitely a switch from life before kiss and after. Needless to say, life after kiss is made of awesome, even though my head is still a little foggy that the whole thing is happening. That this gorgeous, sexy boy likes kissing *me*. That he likes spending time with *me.*

It's like winning the lotto. One of those things that would be cool if it happened, but you never really think it will and then bam! Your whole life changes.

The thing is, it's not just because he's a pretty face either. If that was all, I wouldn't care. I wouldn't want him.

Which I do.

A lot.

But in typical boy fashion, aside from kissing and hand holding, I have no idea if I have him. Are we dating? Is he my boyfriend? Am I the secret girl he likes to lock lips with in private? All these questions circle around in my brain creating a tornado so strong I'm surprised the National Tornado Center doesn't issue an all-points bulletin.

Yes, I'm going that crazy.

Today is a gym day so we didn't jog this morning. Oh, and it also happens to be my weigh in day too. It's weird because I'm not even nervous. Don't get me wrong, I'm hoping I've made some serious progress, but compared to the Tegan Limbo I'm in, I don't have the energy to drive myself crazy, wondering what the number will say, or what he'll think about it.

When I get there, Tegan's waiting for me like always. There's been no kissing on Let's Get Physical premises. I'm not sure if it's because he's embarrassed of me, or because making out with your client probably isn't the most professional thing in the world.

"Hey." Tegan gives me that playful smile of his, one I'm hoping is my smile.

"Hey." He holds the door open for me. This time I walk back to his cubby first, without having to be dragged there.

"Alright, are you ready for this? It's going to be good. I know it. So don't stress, k?" He's standing in front of me in the black shirt with neon green lettering that reads, 'Let's Get Physical'.

"Actually, I'm not..." The extra walk I went on this week pops into my head. The time we spend jogging. The chances I had to cheat while eating and didn't. I've worked hard. *He's* made me work hard and no matter what the numbers say, I'm trying to make myself focus on that.

"Good. Let's measure you first." I fight a shiver when Tegan's finger brushes over my arm longer than necessary as he measures. I don't ask the numbers or look at the numbers, focusing on the way his skin feels against mine as he goes from one arm to the next. To my legs, waist...ok, the waist feels extra nice. Just like when we kiss, all I feel and know is him.

"I hope you're eyes aren't closed because you're freaked out."

My eyes are closed? I pop them open. "No...just tired." Yeah right, hypnotized by his hands is more like it.

"You want the numbers?"

"I don't know, do I?"

"I think you do. Come on. Tell me you do, Annabel Lee."

I love the way he talks to me. How he's always teasing and playful. Plus, it's kind of cool that he has his own name for me and it sounds so hot when he says it. "Please, like I have the willpower in me not to know."

Tegan looks down, then up at me through his thick lashes. His eyebrows raise and lower and then that Tegan smile. "You've lost three inches in your waist alone."

Three inches? *Three inches?* I want to jump up and hug him, but I can't. Not here. Plus, I'm still not brave enough to initiate the physical contact yet, so instead I clap my hands together, holding them at my mouth. "Three inches? Oh my God. That's good right? It seems good."

"Hell yes, it's good! Now gettcha butt on the scale. I have a feeling you're going to be happy with the results there too."

Briefly I wonder if he wants to hug me too. Or kiss me. Does he want to celebrate with me the same way I want to with him? I hope so. Trying to focus on the whole point of this thing, I step onto the scale, watching Tegan's hand as it slides the weight up and down the scale. What? Am I reading this right?

"160.8. All together you've lost five pounds exactly. How does that—umpf!"

This time, I can't help it. I launch myself at him. Tegan catches me, laughing and hugging. It's not record-breaking and I know I still have a long way to go, but holy crap. I've lost six pounds and over three inches!

"Umm, I guess it feels nice and as nice as *you* feel, we have an audience."

I freeze, heat flooding to my cheeks. "Oh, sorry." I pull away from him. "Was just excited."

Tegan winks at me. "It's all good. Come on, let's go get physical."

We are nothing but professional for the whole workout. Tegan pushes me through our leg routine today, counting off each of my pushes or pulls and telling me how good I'm doing. Each time he writes my progress down in his booklet and then we move to the next one.

Is he standing farther away from me than usual? Teasing me less? I'm overreacting. Or am I? Is he upset that I plastered myself against him like I'm a Hillcrest High elite and he's Billy Mason?

"Good workout today and seriously, I'm proud of you," Tegan tells me as we walk to the door. I'm about to tell him thanks and bye when he looks at Supermodel who I now know as Molly and says, "I'm going to take a break. I'll be back in ten, okay?"

Oh no. He's mad. I screwed up and now whatever it was we had going between us is already over. Molly gives him a smile and we walk out. When we get to the parking lot, I throw my bag into the passenger side and close the door, trying to ignore the fact that I know what's coming.

Because it is. The saying "it's too good to be true?" Totally a fact. I lean against my car, crossing my arms like I don't care. I don't. I knew this would happen anyway.

Tegan steps closer to me. Close like always, but he looks nervous. "I was thinking and... well, maybe it's not the best idea for me to be your trainer anymore."

Chapter Fourteen

MY GIRL

"Oh…" I'm not mad at him, I'm mad at me. At the ache in my chest and the fact that even though I said I expected this, it's broken something inside me. "Okay." I turn and try to get into my car which I realize is about the stupidest thing I can do considering it's the passenger side. I don't get far anyway because Tegan stops me.

"Hey, where are you going?"

Is he for real? Like I'm going to sit here while he rattles off a list of why we can't be together or throws the 'it's not you, it's me' line my way. "Home. No need to explain. I understand."

"Um, I'm glad you do, because I don't." Tegan turns me around so I'm facing him again.

"You don't have to do that. I get it. I expected it. I…" You know what? I can't do this. It's not right or not fair. "Actually, I'm pissed. You pretend to like me and then one hug in front of your gym buddies and Supermodel and I'm out the door? Whatever."

"Huh?" he looks at me confused. "I'm not breaking it off with you… You think I would do that because you hugged me?"

He's not breaking up with me. Best news ever! "I just thought."

"That's not me, Annabel Lee—I don't just bail on people. I held your hand all over the zoo and the fair. If I was going to break up with you over a hug, I wouldn't have done that."

My cheeks are hot. Why can't I stop thinking the worst? "Then what do you mean?"

He steps closer, his legs on the outside of mine as his hands grab my waist. I should pull away, but I can't. "I'm not breaking up with you. I'm not mad you hugged me. Actually, I would have liked to do even more with you, but I can't do that here…while you're my client. I need this job too much, or I would."

And his mom told him girls are confusing, I'm thinking that about boys. "Then why?"

Tegan leans forward, pressing his lips to mine too quickly for my taste. "Because." Another kiss. "You're." Oh, one more. "My girl." Two kisses this time. "And it doesn't feel right for you to pay me for us to work out together. Because I want to be able to kiss you when I want and I can't do that if you're my client."

At least I think that's what he said. I'm not sure I caught anything after him telling me I'm his girl. "I am? Your girl, I mean?"

He gives my waist a squeeze and I suck in my stomach. "I thought so, unless you're only using me for my make-out abilities."

"You're so—"

"Conceited. I know. But you like it."

But as much as I like how that sounds, how I want to really be *with* Tegan, thinking about what he said leaves a hole in my chest. I'm not sure I can do this without him. "But what about the money? I know you're saving up to help with college and to help your mom and stuff."

Tegan freezes, his eyes hard on me in a way I've never seen them. "I don't *want* your money. If that's what you think this is about, then we're on a different page here."

I'm such a jerk. I insult the one person who's been nothing but nice to me. Not letting myself be afraid of his reaction, I grab his shirt and pull him back to me. It feels good, this whole control thing. "I'm sorry. I didn't mean that. I just…" He doesn't give me the easy way out, but stands here waiting to hear what I say. "I don't know if I can do it without you."

Tegan sighs. "Don't say stuff like that. You don't need me for anything. This…this is all you. But, I never said you had to do it without me. It's up to you. You want another trainer, I'll hook you up. If not, I am a professional, you know. I can do the same stuff with you if you're not a client that I do now. We can keep jogging together. When we work out here, we'll do it when I'm off the clock and we'll work out *together*. It's not like we can't still use the scales and stuff, so basically it will be the same except you will be my girl working out with me instead of my client who pays me and also happens to kiss me."

The break inside me starts to heal, the heaviness sprouting wings and flying away. This, I can handle. This, I actually like. "Okay. That makes sense. I don't want anyone else, though. I want you."

Tegan smiles. "That's a good thing, because I want you too." Then his face turns serious for a minute. "This is new for me too. It might not seem like it, but it is. I'm not used to being with a girl who I really care about. I hope you know that… that I'm not with you because of what you have or don't have. I'm with you because I like you…the way I feel when I'm with you."

For the second time. It's my lips that find his. "I like you too."

***

I have a boyfriend. A hot boyfriend, but also one that's… pretty incredible too.

I'm still in shock the next day when Em comes over. She has a rare day with no classes and we've decided to spend it together. Of course, she doesn't know I have other options and I feel like the worst friend in world for not telling her, but I know her. She won't understand and I'm already in a state of disbelief that I'm scared her pessimism will make me doubt what's happening.

Which makes me an even worse friend. Who calls their bestie pessimistic? And she would understand and be happy for me, wouldn't she? I wonder how I would feel if it were her. If after years of it only being the two of us, how I would feel if she suddenly had a boyfriend and guess what? My crappy friend status is raised a notch because I would be jealous. But I would also be worried about her, which I know is how she'll feel about me. Right now, I don't want worry. I just want happy.

"Want some ice cream?" Em asks as we sit at her kitchen table. Her house is just as big as mine, but so much homier. The table is small with only four chairs, but half the time she and her mom eat in the living room together while they watch their favorite shows. I like that. Mom and I don't share any shows and while my dad is cool, he's not much of a TV person.

It's on the tip of my tongue to say yes. I mean, hello, it's Cherry Garcia, but then I think about those six pounds and how hard it was to get them off. How easy it would be to put them back on, and like Tegan says, each week will be different. There will be some, where I don't lose, or I only lose one and do I really want to make it worse by cheating now? Nope. "No thanks. I'm not hungry."

She shrugs, scoops herself a bowl and plops down in another kitchen chair. "I can't believe you let your mom do that to your hair."

I'm getting used to it now. It's different, but not too big a deal. "You know how she is, plus, I kind of wanted to try something different."

"You wanted to or you knew she wanted you to?" Em takes a bite of her ice cream.

It's a little of both actually. I wanted something different. Wanted to try and impress Tegan which now that I think about it, is just lame. Like adding some color to a girl's hair is going to change her? And the thing is, I don't really need to change. Not that way at least. Tegan seems to like me the way I am too. But Mom? I know it meant something to her. "What difference does it make?"

"Umm, I'm not even going to dignify that question with a response."

I frown because she's right. "I love that I can always count on you to tell me like it is, Em." *Except when I don't tell you something for that specific reason.*

"That's what I'm here for. You'd do it for me too."

Again I'm hit with a slam of guilt. I'm lying to my best friend in the world. I should tell her. My eyes cast toward the table, I open my mouth to do just that, but she cuts me off. "There's this asshole at the college who won't leave me alone. Every time I turn around he's there. It's driving me crazy."

My head snaps up so I can look at her. Em never talks like that. If there's someone giving her shit, she tells him off, retreats inside herself and that's that. If anyone brings up Billy Mason or any of the other people at school, it's always me. "What did he do to you?" It's funny, but I always thought college would be different. That there, people wouldn't give a shit what other's looked like or if they had a stupid, insignificant birthmark on their face.

"He's just..." She's stirring her ice cream, making Cherry Garcia Soup out of it. "He's always trying to talk to me. Just always there, asking me what I'm listening to on my iPod or if I did the homework. He even tried to *eat* with me the other day."

She gives a look like I'm supposed to agree with her. Tell her what a jerk he is and that she should tell him off. "Well... maybe he's nice? Maybe he likes you."

Emily's eyes and mouth both widen into large "O's". "Please, Bell. You know as well as I do how stuff like that ends. There are hundreds of other girls at the school and he has the urge to talk to the girl in black with the screwed up face? I'm not stupid."

188

"Your face isn't screwed up!" I say even as she rolls her eyes. "I'm serious. It's not that big a deal and maybe he doesn't like the other girls or maybe he thinks you're pretty, or likes black, or you have the same music in common. You never know. Your birthmark doesn't define you, Em. Maybe he's just a good guy and sees that."

Like Tegan? I'm not sure if I would be saying this a few weeks ago. Well, maybe I would have, but I'm not sure I would have believed it.

"Like you don't think you're defined by your weight? Which isn't a big deal, by the way. I mean, you're gorgeous, but do you see it?"

"I..." It's something I can't really answer, because I can pretend all I want that I don't care about my weight. That it's not one of the major things I notice when I look in the mirror. That the first time Tegan says the wrong thing I didn't automatically assume that's where it came from. But the fact is, I'm not there. I'd like to think I'm closer. Maybe that's because of Tegan and our work outs, but I'm still not completely there.

It sucks.

"It's easy to give other people advice, but not always easy to know it yourself, is it?"

I shake my head. "I still think he might like you though."

189

"And I still think he doesn't. I'm happy with you and Mom. I don't need anyone else anyway."

And the worst friend in the world award goes to…. Annabel Conway! Because as much as I need Em, I've found someone else I need too and I'm scared to death to tell her.

**

As I'm driving to Tegan's apartment, my cell phone chirps. I ignore it for a minute because I'm a little lost. He lives in the older side of town with thin streets, cars parked on each side so you have to maneuver between them and you drive down the same street and suddenly it has a different name. I've always wondered what the point in that is? Just call the whole stupid street the same thing. Like I'm not nervous enough about today. The last thing I need is to get lost or to run into a parked car or something.

I look up and see the sign for Hillside Apartment Complex. Just as I'm pulling up, a car pulls away from the curb so I take the spot. It's a medium-sized complex, what looks like a narrow alley running between the buildings with little single car garages attached. It's definitely an older building, but looks nice and well kept.

And I'm stalling by dissecting his apartment. Go, me.

Then I remember my cell and pick it up. It's a text from Tegan.

190

Hey, A. With a client. Running a few minutes late. Go in. Mom's there. See u soon.

Um, no. I love his mom, but the only time I've seen her is pre-kiss. Things feel different now. I don't even know if she knows we're together. It'd just be too uncomfortable. And with a client? I thought he was off today.

That's okay. I can wait outside for u. I reply. It's like five seconds later when my cell beeps again.

Get ur butt in there or I'll send her out for u. She's excited to see u and don't be nervous.

Leave it to Tegan to know I'm nervous. This whole night has me on edge.

Pushing all that thought aside I grab my bag from the passenger seat and get out of the car. It feels like I'm always carrying some kind of bag with my workout stuff nowadays.

It's easy to find which apartment is his. Taking a deep breath, I knock. It takes a few minutes, but then Tegan's mom opens the door. She's wearing a waitress uniform from one of the steak houses in town.

"Hey, sweetie. Come in."

I can't help but smile. I missed her. Dana is pulling a shoe on her foot as she walks, and not doing a good job of it.

"Busy, busy like always." She smiles.

There isn't a lot of furniture in the apartment. I don't know if it's because they can't afford it or because the sparseness probably makes it much easier for Tim to get around. But still, it's cozy. A picture of the three of them hangs over the couch.

"Have a seat. I'm on my lunch break. Just needed to grab something to eat and bring Timmy to a friend's house. What's on the agenda for you guys tonight?" I sit at their dining room table, his mom sitting next to me to finish getting her shoes on. Before I can reply to her, Tim wheels in.

"Ooh, it's Tegan's lover."

"Timothy!" Dana says as my cheeks no doubt turn bright red. "Don't talk like that. You're going to embarrass the poor girl."

"Sorry, Tegan's girlfriend. About time he brought someone around here. I was starting to think he was gay."

"Tim!" This time, it's me who screeches his name. Then of course, I feel like a psychopath.

Tim and Dana both burst into laughter.

"Aw, you don't have to stick up for my brother. You must be just as in looove as he is."

There's a part of me that wants to reply to that, but I'm pretty sure I've lost the ability to use my vocal cords. I'm not in love and Tegan isn't either. That's just ridiculous.

"And she's never going to want to come over again now. Leave her be, Timothy. It's between Tegan and Annabel." She winks. I wonder if she got it from Tegan or he got it from her. "Though it *is* good to see him like someone enough to have some fun. He needs to have more fun. And lucky for us, we love you too."

Nope. Definitely don't have a voice anymore. Might not have a heartbeat either. The sound of the front door opening saves me.

"Speak of the devil." Dana stands up and straightens out her uniform.

"That's me." Tegan closes the door behind him.

Dana smiles. Tegan steps up behind my chair, leans over and kisses me. There's no tongue, just touch of our lips, but it sears me just the same. "Hey, you," he says.

Wondering if my voice will ever come back, I smile.

"You picked up an extra shift today?" he's talking to his mom now.

"Yeah. The extra money doesn't hurt." Tegan shakes his head and his jaw is tense. He hates that his mom has to work so hard. "Did you?" she asks, but he ignores it. "That's not important though. What are you guys up to tonight?"

"Of course it's not. Running yourself into the ground isn't important at all." The room is silent. Usually they get along so well. It's weird to see they're a normal family just like the rest of us.

"Tegan..."

"We're going for a jog, then heading out to a party."

"Timmy's staying with a friend and I won't be home until late. I know you're eighteen, but I'm still your mama and I'm sure I don't have to tell you two to be good, right? No drinking and driving. No other things that will make me a grandma at way too young an age."

Oh. My. God. I think I'm about to die. Is his mom giving us a sex talk?

"Annabel and Tegan. Sitting in a tree," Tim starts. He's way too old for that song, but I know he's giving me a hard time. Especially when Dana sings the KISSING part with him.

"You're such a twerp." Tegan punches Tim in the arm and they start playing around like they did before the basketball practice.

"That's enough boys. I have to go. Timmy, come on. Tegan, I'm serious. Be good."

Yep, I'm dying. *Dying!*

"We'll try." Tegan winks at me and I want to evaporate into thin air.

"Bye, baby." She leans forward and kisses Tegan on the forehead and then to my surprise she does the same to me. "Be good, sweetie. Sorry if I embarrassed you."

I wave her off and they're out the door.

As soon as we're alone, Tegan grabs me and pulls me close. "So...wanna break some rules?"

Chapter Fifteen

LET'S PARTY

I freeze. Is he talking about what I think he's talking about? My body perks at the thought, but my head is pulling on the reigns for me to slow down. What if his mom comes home? What if I make a fool of myself? What if I'm not ready?

"I'm kidding, Annabel Lee. I can't believe you're really thinking about it."

I try and pull away from him, hoping to find someplace to hide.

"No, don't do that. I'm glad you're thinking about it. It's obvious *I* think about it. It's just not what I meant right now."

Laughter dances in his eyes, his lips quirked up in a smile like only Tegan can do. The way he always does, he wipes any tension from the room. I wonder if he knows how good he is at that. If it comes from all the practice he gets trying to make everything perfect for his family. Playfully, I push at his chest, finding it difficult to keep with my original train of thought, because his chest…nice. "So you're conceited *and* perverted!"

He pulls me closer. "I'm multi-talented. What can I say?"

"Ugh! You're a sick, sick person." Wiggling, I try to break free of his arms, but he holds me tight.

"You can't get away from me unless I want you too."

I fight him harder, laughter pouring from my mouth and vibrating us both. Tegan's laughing too, easily pulling me along with him as I try to get away. Then, we're going down. My heart lurches a little, scared we're going to go boom, but he's only dropping back onto the couch and pulling me with him. This is my favorite side of him... when he's just happy. Not working, worried about his mom or feeling guilty over his brother's life. When he doesn't have to hide because he knows there's no pity from me.

"Let me up!" More laughter. "No, I hate to be tickled. Don't tickle me." His hands are at my sides and I'm squirming, but not as much as I could. He feels good. This feels good and even though I could pee my pants right now, I want it to last.

"You didn't say the magic word." Tegan's on top of me, tickling. Through my giggles, I look up, his blond hair is hanging down in his face. I can't help but take him in. He's so beautiful. Not perfect like I first thought. There's the little chip in his tooth, a scar on his face. Gorgeous, yes, but not perfect and that makes me like him all the more.

197

Suddenly he stills. There's no more tickling and he's looking down at me, the way I'm looking up at him. There's a distinct switch in the air from playful to if-I-don't-kiss-you-right-now-I-will-combust. He feels it too. I know it by the way he leans toward me.

"You're kind of addicting, do you know that? I don't know what it is about you, but you're different."

If you could really die from joy, my poor parents would be planning a funeral. But then, if I croaked, I wouldn't be kissing him right now. Wouldn't feel the now familiar press of his lips against mine. The sweep of his tongue as it delves in and out so skillfully. I wouldn't hear the little groan in the back of his throat like I'm driving him wild. *Me.* And he's making me just as crazy.

He kisses the corner of my mouth, my neck, down my throat and then back up to my mouth again. His mom's words start playing through my head. I see her too which is a total buzz kill, making me still.

"What's wrong?" he says, his lips on my collarbone.

"We should slow down... Your mom. The party..." I wish I could pick a sentence and go with it.

He kisses me again, this one quick. "Fine, ruin my fun." Even without the wink, I know he is only teasing me. Tegan stands up, grabs my hand and pulls me up too. "Come on. Let's go work out some of this pent up energy in a less fun, but more productive...Nah, just a less fun way."

***

We head out to our usual jogging spot, stretch and then take the familiar loop. I can jog the whole thing by now. We take it slow, I'm sure he runs much faster without me, but it's still pretty cool that I've passed the point where I have to walk some of it. We do it enough that I know each step now, each turn and I welcome the burn in my legs and lungs. Like Tegan has said before, they're my war wounds, proving to myself that I'm doing what I set out to do. How awesome is that?

And today, I need it. I have a feeling he knows which is why he suggested the run before we go to the party. I've never met his friends and I'm scared to death they're going to take one look at me and wonder what the heck he's thinking. Then, I mentally yell at myself for thinking that way because no matter what, there is nothing wrong with me.

We drive back to Tegan's apartment. I take the shower in his mom's room while he takes the one in the hallway, which let me tell you, it's strange showering in his mom's bathroom. He assured me he okay'd it, but still. The strangeness has nothing on the fact of knowing we're both naked in the same house though, only a wall separating us.

Looks like Tegan isn't the only pervert.

Soon, we're sitting in Tegan's little car on our way to the party. I'm wearing black capris, and a red button-up, summery shirt. The tag said it's slimming, I'm not sure. Tegan's gorgeous as always in his signature shorts, not too baggy, but enough that you can see the edge of his boxer-briefs when he doesn't have a shirt on. I know, because he came out of the bathroom without one. How lucky am I? I'd watched as he pulled a t-shirt over his head, and another short sleeve, button up, over it, left open.

"It might be a little wild there, but not bad wild. They're cool people. You'll have fun."

"Cool." I'm annoyed that I'm so nervous, but happy I'm going regardless. That counts for something, right?

"Are you sure you wanna go? We can hit up a movie or something. Head back to my house, whatever. I don't want you to go if you don't want to." His eyes are on the road, but mine are on him.

"No. I want to. I do. I'm just being a dork."

"You are kind of dorky." Tegan laughs.

"And you like me so what does that say about you?"

"That I'm lucky." I don't reply to that. We're parking in front of a big house out in the boonies. I guess the guy's aunt and uncle own it and they're out of town. He doesn't turn off the engine. "Seriously, though. Do you want to do something else? We can hang out with your friend, Emily if you want. I'm up for anything. It just feels good to be doing something."

Everything he says or does makes me like him more. He said he's lucky? I think I'm the lucky one. Or actually, maybe both of us. "I do want to go, Tegan. I just get nervous. I haven't really done the whole party thing. The people at my school are jerks, so this is all just new to me. I don't want to back out though. I want to have fun and meet your friends."

He sighs. "You know, one of these days, you're going to have to tell me what happened. Who hurt you, but for now, I'm stoked because I really want to have some fun with you tonight. I haven't gone to a party or anything in a long time."

And he's right, I do, but not now.

***

The house is swimming with people. Tegan and I have a hard time weaving through the crowd, but he doesn't let go of my hand once. A few people say hi to him as he leads us through the sea. "We're headed downstairs!" He has to yell over the crowd and music so I can hear him. "Rick and Bo said they'd be down there playing pool."

Instead of trying to fight the noise, I nod my reply. Tegan presses a quick kiss to my lips and starts to walk again. Will I ever get used to that? I'm really not sure I want to lose the excitement. We find the stairs that leads us down to a game room, complete with a pool table, air hockey, big screen TV, and a wrap-around couch. There are a couple guys playing air hockey. At a pool table, two girls and two guys are playing doubles.

They all look like Tegan. Well, not as good looking as he is, but they dress like him and you can tell they're the type who were popular in school. The girls? They're all wearing skirts, tight shirts and look way, *way* different from me.

"Holy shit! Tegan's here. We didn't think your workaholic ass would actually show up!" One of the guys yells, beer in his hand. Everyone turns to look at us. I try to smile, hoping I don't look as nervous as I feel. Tegan's squeeze on my hand helps.

"Whatever, douchebag. Just because some of us work and have plans doesn't mean you need to talk crap." They're laughing. Tegan lets go of my hand long enough to bump knuckles with a few of the guys and then he's holding me again.

"Hey! I work. I just have a life too which up until tonight, you haven't had for a while." The guy looks at me. "Hey, you must be Annabel. I'm Bo."

I'm not even embarrassed to admit, I'm doing a little squeal inside. It's cool that Tegan has told these people about me and it soothes my nerves a bit. "Nice to meet you."

Another guy comes over, wearing a baseball hat. "What's up, Teag."

"What's up. This is my girlfriend, Annabel. Annabel Lee, this is Rick. The girl behind him is his girlfriend, April and," he points to the other girl at their pool table, "that's Sandra." April smiles and gives me a wave. She has red hair and kind eyes. Sandra's blonde and says hi too.

"Good job getting Tegan out of the house. He's been a hermit lately," Sandra says.

Their words surprise me. I know his mom said he focuses on work a lot and I know that's because he helps her and is saving for school, but hermit seems pretty heavy. "Thanks, but he's usually the one dragging me around." They seem nice, smiling at me as I speak. Pretty soon Bo's dragging them all back to the table to finish the game and I'm standing against the wall with Tegan watching them.

The game ends quickly afterward. They ask us if we want to play and both Tegan and I say no, so they start a second game. "Want to share a beer with me?" he asks. I'm not much of a beer girl so I tell him no. He comes back with one for himself and a bottle of water for me. A few people come by and talk to Tegan here and there. He introduces me each time and I'm surprised I haven't gotten any double takes. No strange looks. Nothing.

Tegan finishes his beer and sets it on a table, leaning against the wall, he pulls me against him. My arms find their way around his neck, as he's holding my waist, brushing his fingers back and forth.

"Not so bad, huh," he whispers against my ear.

Truthfully, I say, "Not at all."

"I knew you'd have fun. My friends are all pretty kickback."

"I thought you said they're wild."

"It's different. They like to have fun and in a few hours, they'll be a little crazier than they are now, but they're cool too. Kickback, just like to have fun and hang out. And they like you. I can tell." He kisses by my ear, teasing his way down my jaw line. "I'm not the only one with good taste."

I laugh him off, but inside I'm glowing. He's always saying stuff like this to me and I never say it back. Never say it first. I'm not sure why. "I'm the one with good taste. I kind of like you, you know?"

"Only kind of?" He holds me tightly against him.

"Maybe a little more than kind of."

"I knew it!" Tegan's lips slide toward mine, but before they hit their destination, we're interrupted.

"Tegan! Get your love-struck ass over here and play a game with us. The girls are done and Mike wants to play so we need someone else for doubles."

"I'm busy," Tegan tells Rick.

I remember how excited his friends were to see him. How they say he hasn't hung out much lately. "You should go play. I don't mind watching."

He gets a little light in his eyes and I know he wants to go play, but was nervous about leaving me. "You sure?"

"Absolutely. Unlike someone, I'm not a hermit."

He gives me a quick peck.

I watch him head over to the pool table. It isn't but a few seconds later that I hear, "Come sit with us, Annabel." It's April. She and Sandra are sitting on the couch alone. Without the hesitance I would expect, I walk over and sit by them. The boys are laughing at the table, making fun of each other and playfully pushing when one of them make a shot. It's so funny how at ease guys can be together. It's so different from girls, I think. They can be friends with anyone and it's normally not like that with us. Which sucks. Luckily, I don't seem to have to worry about that tonight.

"How long have you guys been together?" Sandra asks, examining her fingernails. It's weird because it doesn't feel like she's ignoring me or not interested in what I'm saying, where with someone else, the gesture might come off that way.

"Um… a couple weeks? Not too long."

April turns to face me. "Oh, I love how you met stories. Where did you guys meet?"

Oh joy! This is where I get to explain that Tegan is helping me lose weight. So not the romantic story I'm sure she's expecting…but then, it does kind of feel that way to me. I never would have expected it, but I like our story. "We met at the gym he works at. I am—was a client of his…"

206

"Oh, Tegan's getting hot and heavy at work. I never would have thought it possible. Now we know why he's such a workaholic, he's there to see you!" April teases and I can't help but like her train of thought.

"No, remember we haven't been together very long."

"Yeah, but it's more fun to think it's because of you. He's so determined. So much different than he was a few years ago."

I realize they all mean before the accident. Briefly, I wonder what he was like back then. Would I have still liked him? Would he have still liked me? "It's funny because you guys keep talking about him working all the time. His mom mentioned it too, but I don't see it. I mean, he's taken time off and we went to watch his brother play basketball and we've gone out a few times. We jog a lot too. He seems too full of life to be that way."

Sandra stops playing with her nails and looks at me. "He likes to have a good time. He always has been like that: fun, funny, outgoing and he still is, he just feels so much responsibility I think. He's been such a homebody since the accident."

I say, "Yeah, he's a good guy." My eyes find their way to him, watching him concentrate on a shot. "He cares about everyone. Wants to do what he can for everyone in his life." His hair falls down in his face and he shakes it out of the way, eye on the ball, then briefly looks up and winks at me.

It's almost like a touch, my skin pebbling as though his fingers are ghosting against it.

"Oh, girlfriend. You have it bad. I mean, who wouldn't and it's obvious he's in love with you too."

I'm not sure if it's April or Sandra who talks because I can't pull my eyes away from the totally hot guy who is my boyfriend. Somehow I should set them straight. We're not in love, it hasn't been very long, but the words lodge in my throat.

"I know, right? He's totally into her. So different than he was with Pammie."

That catches my attention. My eyes shift to the girls again. "Who's Pammie?"

It's April who replies. "This other girl who hangs out sometimes. They hooked up a few times, nothing serious, but he broke it off. She's still got it bad for him, but that's Pammie. She likes to be the one who does the dumping rather than the other way around and he was never serious about her, so don't worry."

Actually, I didn't even think of it to worry until she told me *not* to worry. Funny how that works. Tegan doesn't give me much time to think about it because he walks up to us. "You win?" I ask.

He's standing right in front of me, my eyes level with his...well, his crotch. And again his pervertedness is rubbing off on me because I kind of want to stare.

"Do you have to ask?"

"Of course not. I should have known, big head."

"That's what I love about you, Annabel Lee. You're always so sweet to me." I start to choke on...well, air I guess. Or shock. Can you choke on shock?

"She looks like she's about to pass out." Sandra starts fanning me. I like these girls. I like them a lot. Which makes me think about Em and wish she were here with me. Wish she could meet them too. I never would have thought it coming here, but this night has been perfect.

"Dude, I forgot to tell you, I saw your dad the other day." Bo says as he walks up and Tegan freezes. Bo doesn't seem to notice because he continues. "He had some chick with him. I swear she couldn't have been older than twenty-two. Your dad's got game!"

Now it's Tegan who looks like he's going to pass out. I've seen him upset, but never, *ever* anything like the lost, angry look clouding his eyes right now.

"Yeah…good for him." He's trying to play it off with a shrug, but I see the dents in his armor, I just don't know what to do about it.

"How's he doing anyway? Tim?" This time it's Rick who asks.

I'm not sure if Tim is a safer subject or not—not when knowing his dad left because he couldn't take Tim's injury.

"I'm gonna go grab a drink, I'll be back." I reach for Tegan's hand, but he kind of shakes it off and then he disappears into the crowd. Everyone around me keeps talking so I assume they didn't notice, but I do and it doesn't feel good. I get it, he's angry, but why can't I be there for him the way he is for me?

We talk for about fifteen more minutes, but I can't stop thinking about Tegan. The girls and I exchange phone numbers and I'm excited to have met new friends. Friends I *will* introduce to Emily. It hurts too much to keep her out of this part of my life, but I can't enjoy it now. My mind is with him.

"I'm going to find Tegan." They tell me goodbye and walk away.

Soon I'm sifting through people again on my way to the kitchen. As soon as I round the corner, he's there. Not looking at me and not alone. "It was good seeing you, Pammie. But I gotta get back. My girl's waiting for me downstairs." The only reason I can hear him is because we're in a hallway, him at one end and me at the other. It's empty and though there's music, he's speaking loudly for her to hear and enabling me to hear too. But I don't really give a crap about why or how I can hear him. What I do care about is, Pammie is hot. Like hot enough that she takes my breath away.

Skinny. Super skinny, short skirt I'd get kicked out of school for wearing, pierced belly button. How do I know, you might ask? Oh, because her shirt is practically non-existent. Nice. She has black hair like me. Only hers is long and glamorous and I want to chop it off.

But then…he'd said his girl is downstairs. His girl being *me*. There's a Pepsi in one of his hands and a bottle of water in the other. For *me*. It all should make me feel better, but it doesn't. How can I ever compete with her? *Maybe I don't have to…*

"Yeah, I saw you with her. I thought you didn't want a relationship? I thought you had too much on your plate to be with anyone?"

"I do have a lot I'm dealing with and I didn't want a relationship, but things change. Not that it's any of your business."

"So things changed because of *her?* You can do so much better, Tegan. We look much better together."

I feel as though someone has socked me in the gut. I can hardly breathe.

"No thanks and on that note, I'm out. And don't ever say anything about her again." Tegan tries to walk around her, but she stops him, a hand on the same chest I touched earlier.

"Wait...I..." And then she leans forward and kisses him. Her lips. *My* boyfriend. It's only a couple seconds. Everything in me breaks. I want to run. I should run. It hurts too bad to see this, because she's right. They *do* look good together. But you know what? I don't care. And as much as the instinct to run rears inside me. I don't. Not away at least. I run toward them, because this boy is mine and I'm not going down without a fight.

Chapter Sixteen

THE RETURN OF ROCKY

Before I reach them, Tegan's already pushing her away. The drinks hit the floor, liquid going everywhere. "What the hell, Pammie?!"

Later I'll realize I had time to stop myself, but in this moment, it doesn't feel like it. My hands are out and I push her. "Yeah, what the hell?" Okay, I'm sure this doesn't strike you as a shock, but me? I'm not the fighting kind of girl. Right now? I could totally box with her. Maybe give her a taste of my right hook that Tegan's always talking about.

"Um, excuse you, bitch, but you better not push me again."

"Um, excuse *you*, bitch, but you better not kiss my boyfriend again." The little Annabel Angel on my shoulder is shocked. I am too, but it doesn't stop me. I've been pushed around too much in my life.

"And what are you going to do about it if I do?" People are starting to fill the hallway. Pammie looks around, noticing. "You're delusional if you think he really wants *you*."

Tegan cuts in. "Shut up, Pammie. You don't know what you're talking about." Tegan reaches for me. "Come on, baby. Let's go."

But I can't. I pull myself out of his reach. "You're delusional if you think throwing yourself at a guy who dumped you and kissing him will make him want you." There! Take that!

"Screw you!" Pammie comes at me to push me. I have no clue where it comes from, but I manage to dodge her and push her instead. She slips in the spilled soda Tegan dropped and ends up on her butt in the middle of the hallway. Everyone around us starts laughing except Tegan, me and Pammie. She's pissed, I have no idea what Tegan's thinking and I'm in shock. Twice, I just pushed this girl. I don't condone fighting, but it feels good not to back down. To push back when someone attacks me.

"You pushed me, you stupid, fat cow. What are you going to do? Sit on me next?"

The hall goes dead quiet. Probably not in reality, but for me, it does. I hear nothing except for her words and suddenly, I feel stupid. What am I doing here?

"Watch. Your. Mouth," Tegan seethes at her. "There's nothing wrong with Annabel."

"Annabel? Isn't that a cow name? Even her parents knew she'd be a lard ass."

They're so close to words I've heard from Billy before.

I have nothing left inside me.

No words.

No fight.

Shoving my way through the crowd, I run.

***

"Annabel Lee. Wait up."

I burst through the front door, ignoring Tegan. As soon as my feet hit the porch, I'm running again. I need to get to his car. Need to get out of here.

"Annabel. Wait for me."

He's right behind me when I get to his car. My eyes start to sting as he looks at me with kindness. "She's a bitch. She doesn't know what she's talking about and I'm so sorry—"

"Not now," I shake my head. "I can't talk about it yet. Just…get me out of here."

He nods, opening the door for me. I get in and a second later we're driving. Not toward his house, but he could take me anywhere right now and I wouldn't care. We end up at the beach. A look out spot that thankfully, is deserted. Which ironically enough, is just how I feel. Barren. Alone. I know it doesn't make sense. I tell myself to just get over it. Who gives a crap what that girl says? But my heart and head are heading in different directions. My brain's floating ashore while my heart drifts out to sea.

"You know I think you're beautiful, right? That I don't give a shit about any of the other stuff. I just like spending time with you."

His words are my life boat. He throws them out to me and my instinct is to grab on, to let myself float to safety on them. Tegan always knows how to make me feel buoyant, as though just by him thinking I'm beautiful, that because he likes to be with me, I could make it to shore without the boat. But what happens when he's not here? He can't always be here.

"You're way too strong to let her drag you under, Annabel Lee. You have to know that."

Tegan's right. To a degree at least. And even though I know he can't always be here, he's here now and I intend to take advantage of that. To ride his waves, and hope that later I'm able to stand up on the surfboard without him. "I'm trying to be. I want to be." How he manages to pull such truth out of me, so much feeling, I don't know, but it feels good not to hide. To step out from my secret hiding place and say, *"Here I am! Look at me! This is how I feel"* even if it means getting tagged "it".

"Sometimes I think I'm stronger than I am and other times, I know my weaknesses. It's hard to find that middle ground. To accept my weaknesses without embracing them as a part of me I can never change." My words are even confusing me. It makes sense in my head, but not out loud. "Do you know what I mean or do I just sound like a psycho?"

"Well… maybe not psych-ward crazy, but a little confusing."

I can't believe it, but I almost smile. "How do you always know the right thing to say?"

Tegan's thumb makes feather-soft circles on my cheek and I lean into him. "I don't. Half the time I'm scared as hell I'm saying the dumbest shit in the world." More softness. More circles. "You know, it might come as a surprise to you, but I'm not always as sure as I like to come off. I have a lot of stuff I'm trying to work through too."

"I know..." I remember how he looked at Bo and Ricks words tonight. Knowing his dad left and all he does to try and hold his family together. Yes, Tegan is a little broken like me.

"You wanna talk about it?"

"I think I need to."

"K. Hold up a sec." Tegan gets out of the car, comes around opens my door for me. I think we're going to go outside, but he pulls me in the backseat with him. His arm comes around me and I let my back rest against the side of his chest. Even though it's warm, even with the windows down, Tegan's heat is welcoming.

"I feel stupid even talking about it. I mean, people get teased all the time."

"That doesn't make it hurt any less for the person on the receiving end."

Like always, he's right. "You know how it goes. There's always someone at school who gets it. We've talked about it before. How shitty school is."

It's hard talking about this and keeping my emotions out of it. I want to, I need to, but then I don't, do I? I should be able to share this with Tegan.

I nuzzle closer to him. In return, he squeezes me tighter. "On the last day of school last year, I knew something was up. Everyone was staring at me more than usual. Snickers, laughs, pointing. Em noticed it too, but we tried to blow it off. I mean, we didn't usually care what people thought about us.

"About halfway through the day, I started hearing little comments. *Fat Girl in Love.* Little digs about how stupid I was. How delusional I was. I seriously had no idea what was happening."

My eyes are watering now. Tears are dripping down my face, rolling down my neck. Tegan reaches over and catches them.

"So it's the end of the day. We're in the commons. Everyone's there, all hyped up because school's out for the summer. That's when this guy—Billy Mason—comes up to me and shoves a letter in my hand. I swear, I think the whole school was around us, Tegan. I felt *everyone's* eyes on me while I read it."

I take a few breaths, forcing myself to continue. "It was a love letter. A love letter from me that I didn't write. It was made out to Billy. Everyone had a copy. They were all holding them, reading and laughing at all the things they thought I said to Billy. We worked together for our final in English so whoever wrote it took the idea from that. It spelled out how I fell in love with him while working with him, how gorgeous I thought he was. How nice he was to me."

I try to pull away, needing a little space, but he holds me tighter. That's when I realize I don't need the space after all. I need him.

"Needless to say, I denied it. Also needless to say, Billy played it up. How he just felt bad for the fat girl and he didn't mean for me to fall in love with him. That he gets it—how a girl like me would want to think there could be something between us, but I'm not his type. How I'm such a nice girl, but he likes his girls with a little less meat on their bones. Everyone loved that one."

I shake my head. "The more I denied it, the more they seemed to think it was real. He kept telling me I didn't have to be in denial. They all saw the letter, crap like that. It was so embarrassing, Tegan. I hated him, but I hated me too."

"No." He pulls away so we can look at each other. "You have nothing to hate yourself about. That's bullshit, Annabel Lee. He's the jerk. There's nothing wrong with you."

"There's the part of me that knows it, but it doesn't make it any easier to deal with. It doesn't make it hurt any less."

More tears are coming. Tegan pulls me against him and I cry into his chest. It feels good leaning on him. Having him here for me. Trusting him in a way I've never done with anyone. When all the tears are gone, he tilts my head up and places a soft kiss to my lips.

"First of all, Billy would be honored to have you love him. I have to admit, I'm pretty stoked you don't. Makes me luckier because you're mine."

This time I really do smile.

"Second, I'm sorry that happened to you. High school sucks. It won't be like that in college. Only three more semesters for you and you'll be done."

Another kiss.

"And third, I'm totally going to kick Billy's ass if I ever see him."

I know he's only saying that to make me feel better, and it works. I do.

"I guess it's my turn now…you know, the whole opening up thing…"

There's something about his voice, I can tell he doesn't want to. That he's not ready yet, so I try to lighten the moment the way he always does for me. "Or… we can just make-out instead. Unless—"

My words are cut off by his lips. I'm guessing he'd rather make-out.

Chapter Seventeen

BUSTED

It's been two weeks since my little confession to Tegan and I haven't regretted it once. I feel like I've cleared the air and I'm one step closer to becoming the person who doesn't need to run. Who would have told Pammie where she could stuff it when she brought my weight into it.

The cool part? It has nothing to do with the twelve freaking pounds I've lost since the beginning of the summer. Yep, that's right, twelve. There's a part of me who wishes I could have dropped more, who feels like I'm losing weight slower than a grandma drives, but from everything I've read, that's the way to do it. That's what Tegan says. If you drop it too quickly, you'll gain it back, I'm building lean muscle. Yada, yada. I'm not going to lie, I kind of tune out some of that stuff. I'm trying to focus on the part of me that realizes I've lost twelve freaking pounds and that's pretty kick butt if you ask me.

Eighteen more and I'll be at my target. One thirty-five. A number I haven't seen for years. One that Mom would probably hire a trainer if she ever hit, but for me, it's perfect.

I'm leaning against a pole while Tegan's doing his round of biceps. We rotate now, him and me, working out together. It's like a partnership and I love it. The view isn't so bad either.

"What are you smiling at over there?" He lets go of the bar.

"You."

"Because I'm so hot?"

"Because you're not a grunter."

One of Tegan's eyebrows rises. "Aw, you're so sweet. Wait till I tell the guys my girl doesn't think I'm a grunter."

I snap him with my towel. "Shut up. I mean, some of the guys in here are all loud and grunt when they lift. I think they do it so people look at them, which I don't understand, but I'd wondered about you. If you'd be a grunter and now I know you're not."

He shakes his head. "You're so weird, but I still love you."

Defibrillator anyone? Jumper cables? I'll go for anything to help jump start my heart right now. Does he mean *love* me, love me or is it just one of those passing comment things? Passing comment. It has to be, but all of a sudden, it's really hot in here. I'm feeling a little dizzy like I have a bad case of heat stroke. What if he means it? Does he really love me? I mean, we're young. He starts college in September and though it's local and I plan to be there in a year, would it be smart to go falling in love right now?

"Breathe, Annabel Lee." Tegan stand ups, snickering and then leans close to my ear. Will he say it again? Am I supposed to say it back? Gah, Holy heart attack in the making. Closer he comes and my nerves are seizing.

"Come on. We still have abs to do and then I have to clock in."

Did I mention I really want to know if he really loves me? Because I'm kind of scared that I'm more than halfway in love with him.

***

I spoon steamed vegetables onto my plate, cut the piece of chicken in half because it's huge and I don't need that much anymore, and add a small amount of red potatoes. It's a healthy meal, none of it fried or anything, not that Mom's ever been big on frying, but I know just by eating less, I'm doing something good for myself. The part that rocks even more is that I'm full after this amount of food. I don't understand why I ever thought I needed more than this.

Mom's late to the table, coming in after my and Dad's plates are made. Surprisingly, there's no phone with her. Instead she's looking at Dad and he's looking back at her and I know something's up.

"What's wrong?" All sorts of thoughts are going through my head. Divorce, sickness. I choose to ignore the fact that I automatically go to worst case scenarios.

"I ran into Emily today." Mom's voice is tight, angry.

"What happened? Is she okay?"

It's Dad who replies. "Pumpkin, she said she hasn't seen much of you lately. Your mother commented about your staying out with her a couple times and asked about the movies, but she had no idea what she was talking about."

Holy crap. Leave it to me to finally get a life and get caught lying about it.

"Of course she tried to cover, but the damage was done. What have you been doing, Annabel?" Mom doesn't sound nearly as understanding as dad.

"I…"

"Why were you lying? Are you on drugs? You're leaving the house early every morning, and you look thinner. Are you on something?"

It's sad that a little part of me does a cheer that she noticed. It's like a compliment she's issued even though she's accusing me of doing drugs to lose weight at the same time. But she's noticed and it feels better than it should.

"Drugs, Paulette? You can't be serious."

"You always defend her! Always try and make me the bad guy."

I want to plug my ears so I don't hear their fighting. It's me. Always about me. "Of course I'm not on drugs!" The only reason I raise my voice is so they'll hear me.

"Then who are you with? Why have you lied about where you are?" Then, a light bulb goes off in Mom's eyes and I realize she knows. This shouldn't bother me, but it does. They'll burst mine and Tegan's bubble. Both him and what I'm doing won't be mine anymore. It will be theirs to dissect and question me about.

To my surprise, she then shakes her head. "No, it couldn't be a boy."

Pain pierces my chest. My eyes sting. Anger and hurt wrestle inside me. My heart jumps when Dad's hands come down on the table, shaking the glasses.

"You always do this to her. Why can't it be a boy? Because she's not you? Because she doesn't spend three hours with her face in the mirror every day?"

Mom pushes to her feet. "I always do this to her? You always do this to me. You're always putting words in my mouth so you're her savior and I'm the witch. I only meant that she wouldn't keep a boy from me. That's something a daughter shares with her mom."

I don't even have it in me to feel guilty. I can't believe she thinks I would share it with her. We never talk about anything that matters.

"So you think she'd be on drugs before she might keep something from you? Hell, Paulette, all she did is lie about where she was. All teenagers do it."

Back and forth they yell about me. Fight about me. They think they know who I am. What I do. What's best for me. Their voices are an echo, a muffled echo beating against my brain until I can't take it anymore. I'm pushing to my feet. My chair falls backward on the floor. "Enough! I can't do this! Stop fighting about me like I'm not here!"

It hurts to breathe, to talk, but I keep going. "I joined a gym and got a trainer because I'm tired of being fat. He's the only person who lets me be me. Who isn't telling me what I need to do, offering me makeovers, defending me, or trying to fix me—which is funny since he started out as my trainer. But it has always been about what I want and now he's my boyfriend and that's who I'm with every day. And I lied so I could avoid *this*!"

The room is dead quiet. As always Mom looks perfect, regal in her royal room. She's almost too calm. Me? I'm a live-wire, thrashing around because I'm not sure I did the right thing. Not sure I should have told them anything.

There's a long silence before Dad speaks. "Wow… I'm…I'm in shock here." He shakes his head, confused, "I'm sorry if you feel like we expect certain things of you, Pumpkin. You're mother and I might not always show it in the right way, but we love you. Isn't that right, Paulette?" As always, it's Dad who understands. Dad who gets it.

Mom doesn't. "I want to meet him. Invite him to dinner, Annabel."

Nausea churns in my stomach. I don't want Tegan to meet her. I don't want him to see me through her eyes. "Why?"

"You say this boy is a trainer? At the gym?"

Oh. Now, I get it. She doesn't think I'm good enough for him. What would a boy who likes to work out want with me? It hurts so much, all of it that I can't hold it back any longer. "So you haven't even seen him and he's too good for me? Just like the pageant was too good for me too? What if I *wanted* to do it, Mom?" I'm not yelling because I don't have it in me. I just really want to know. I need to know.

She sighs. "Annabel, I never said he's too good for you and the pageant... You wouldn't have wanted to do it anyway."

"What is she talking about, Paulette?" Dad interrupts.

"They had an open space and asked if Annabel would like to participate. I know our daughter, so I told them no. End of story."

I try to talk past the shake of my chin. "You *lied* and told them I wasn't available. You thought it would embarrass me? Why would it embarrass me if it's not because I'm not pretty enough? If I'm not skinny or perfect enough?"

"Oh, Pumpkin. You're beautiful. You have to know that. Both your mother and I think so."

Mom looks from Dad, to me. "Of course, I'm the bad guy again. You're completely twisting what I said, Annabel. Now if you'll excuse me, I have a phone call to make."

Without another word, she walks out of the room and I'm on the floor in a heap, tears finally falling from my eyes. Dad's arms come around me, trying to comfort me, but it makes me cry more. I start mumbling. I don't get why she hates me. Why she'll never love me. All I want is to be enough for her.

"Shh, pumpkin. Your mom doesn't hate you and you *are* enough. Don't you ever think otherwise."

I hadn't realized I spoke out loud. With the heel of my hand, I try and wipe my tears away, but more keep falling.

"She doesn't know how to express herself very well. She just shuts down, but that's not your fault. It's something she needs to work on, but none of this is your fault. I'm damn proud of you, kiddo, and she is too. I'll talk to her. I'll fix it."

For the first time, I realize he doesn't get it. He doesn't understand me. My poor dad doesn't understand her either.

I pull away, shoving the tears aside. "Daddy, I love you so much, but I don't want you to fix it. Don't you see? You're always trying to make things easier on me and as much as I appreciate it, I have to do it for myself."

Dad frowns, and I notice the wrinkles around his mouth for the first time. "Do I do that? Make you feel inferior? That's never been my intention."

As much as it kills me to hurt him, I have to be honest. He might be the only person in this world beside Tegan that I feel comfortable enough to be honest with right now. "I'm sorry, Daddy. I know you didn't mean it."

I'm shocked with the intensity of his hug as he pulls me close to him. "You have nothing to be sorry about. I love you and I believe in you and I hope you know I never wanted to make you feel like I didn't think you could take care of yourself. I'm not sure if you realize it, but I think you can do just about anything in this world, Annabel."

Then I'm squeezing him just as tight as he's squeezing me. Eventually I'm going to have to stand up to Mom, talk to Em, but right now, all that matters is Dad and me. I've crossed my milestone and there's no one else I'd rather have holding me at the finish line.

"Your mom... she's built differently than we are emotionally, but I promise, she does love you."

I nod pretending I believe him. He needs me to believe him because he loves us both.

"But I do agree with your mother on one thing. I want to meet the boy who's special enough to catch your attention."

Chapter Eighteen

FIGHTING WITH WORDS HURTS MORE THAN FISTS

Talking to Em will be much easier than talking to Mom. At least that's what I tell myself when I text her that we need to talk. She replies right away and I arrange to pick her up.

"Hey," she mumbles when she climbs into my car. The slight catch in that one little word tells me how hurt she is. How left behind she feels because she knows something is up. That I've been doing something without her while using her for an excuse. The word 'hey' vibrates through me, causing little waves of guilt to ripple inside.

She doesn't ask where we're going and I don't offer. I know Em and right now, she's not up for small talk. Or maybe I'm just being all cowardly lion because I'm honestly freaked out to talk to her. What if she doesn't understand? What if I've ruined the friendship that has saved me so many times because I've turned into a liar? A shudder rips through me because if it happens, I probably deserve it. Em doesn't need many people in her life, but I know she needs me. By cutting her out of this, she's going to think I don't need her in the same way.

Instead of bringing her to our spot, I bring her to mine and Tegan's jogging place. I know he's at work, so he won't be here and I don't want to risk another 'near Billy experience' like we had at the pond last time. Without a word she gets out of the car. I follow, walking to the little hideaway Tegan and I found.

"So? What's up? I've been downgraded from BFF to your excuse to go hang out with whoever you hang out with now?" Her hood is up and she's facing away from me, sitting on top of a picnic table.

My heart is going crazy the way it did on those first runs with Tegan, but for a totally different reason. "You'll always be my best friend, Em." I sit beside her. "I just... I know it sounds stupid and probably makes no sense, but I just needed to keep this to myself for a while. I needed to navigate it on my own without anyone else telling me what to do."

"First, I don't even know what *this* is. You still haven't taken the time to tell me and second, when do I ever tell you what to do?"

I can do this. I need to do this. "It's not that you really tell me what to do, it's just…I know you would have tried to talk me out of it and I wasn't sure I wanted to be talked out of it. I know you care about me, Em. I know you don't want me hurt, but you're always there to defend me against Billy. You're telling me guys are jerks and never to trust them. You're telling my mom where to stick it and I love you for it, but this time…I just didn't want to be told I didn't have to make changes. I didn't want you to tell me not to trust him. I was scared to death I'd fall on my face, but I think I needed to take that chance on my own."

"Of course it has to be a guy. I should have known, and since when does sticking up for a friend make me a shitty person?"

"Hey," I turn so I'm looking at her. "Don't do that. I never said you were a shitty friend. I just needed to do something for me. Maybe to prove to myself I can? Maybe because I was already scared to death that I couldn't do it, that he would hurt me and I didn't want to share that with anyone. I don't know, Em. Maybe it just made it more real, but Tegan. He's…"

"So is that why you didn't want me to meet him? Because your new boyfriend is making you work out because he doesn't think you're good enough and he might want me to get a new face, too?"

Anger shoots through me. "I know you're hurt, but that's not fair. Tegan wants to meet you. He's asks about you so much and he would never make me work out. He likes me the way I am. He's not the judgmental type, Em, I swear it. He's amazing. So amazing that I think…" I've hidden so much from my friend lately that I can't hide this. There's no one else I want to share it with. "I think I love him."

Emily freezes. No movement. I'm not even sure she's breathing, but then I see her eyes glistening with the familiar shimmer of unshed tears. Suddenly, she pushes to her feet. "Good for you, Bell. You be in love with your non-judgmental boyfriend and keep on forgetting about me. I can't help but wonder though, if you weren't worried about what Mr. Perfect would think of me, that maybe you just didn't want another dirty mark on your reputation. You're already freaked out about your weight so I guess you didn't want to add a screwed up friend into the mix, too."

Despite the heat and the anger simmering inside me, ice begins to slither through my veins. My eyes are starting to tear up now too. Shame, guilt, confusion all tying me up. That's not true, is it? Was I subconsciously embarrassed of my own best friend? No. No, it can't be. But maybe it is? I'm not sure I knew it, but she might be right. What kind of person am I? "Em--" My voice cracks and I don't finish, at a loss of what to say.

"No worries, Annabel. I get it." She crosses her arms and looks down. "I'd like you to take me home now."

***

"Come on, slow poke. I'm leaving you in the dust back there. I thought we were going on a jog, not a walk."

I push myself forward, trying to catch up with Tegan. The fact is, I'm not into it. It's been two days since my blow-up with Em. Three since the fight with Mom and I don't have the guts to talk to either of them. I'm not sure I deserve to ever talk to Em again and my heart can't take being steamrolled by Mom, because as much as I'd like to think I've grown, as much as I say I want to do things on my own and stand up for myself, there's a part of me that still knows I can't. Not with her.

"We can't all be as good as you, Gym Boy." I'm so shocked at the words that fall from my mouth that I don't realize Tegan has stopped running and I slam into the back of him. "Ouch! Warn a girl, would ya."

He turns to face me, his hair all windblown and messy. "We're back to that now? Calling me Gym Boy? What's wrong?"

"Nothing." *Everything.*

"Don't play games with me, Annabel. I think we're past that. What's wrong?"

Like always, I can't help myself from leaning on him. For the past month and a half, I've done a lot of leaning on Tegan. Too much? I'm not sure, but right now, I need him. Before I know what I'm doing, I'm a blubbering mess. Tears, those big gasping cries that are *not* cute are echoing through the park and he's walking, arm around me, to sit me down. Thank God it's a deserted area, because I can't hold myself back from spilling it all. I tell him about dinner, Mom, Dad, Em. How I'm the worst friend in the world and how much I miss her. How scared I am to confront Mom. Everything. I even tell him about the pageant. Tegan doesn't say a word, letting my verbal river of words break through the dam.

Finally after the hiccup crying is complete and the story told he speaks. "You're not a bad friend. You love Em. No one's perfect. I'm not sure you weren't embarrassed of her at all, but if you were...I get it."

Not him. He doesn't screw up, I want to say, but I don't. "She hates me."

"She doesn't hate you. She loves you. She's worried about you and she'll forgive you, just like you'll forgive her. Emily isn't completely innocent here either."

How is it he always makes me feel better? That his words are like law to me? *Because I'm still not standing on my own. I'm still doing the right things for the wrong reasons and I need to learn how to be strong without Tegan.* "She'll forgive me?"

"Of course." He wraps his arms around my waist and pulls me closer. "But you know that. You don't need me to tell you half the stuff I do. I'm not sure why you think so, but you know it all right here," he touches my head like he did all those weeks ago when he said I needed to believe I could lose weight. "And here." He touches my heart again. "When are you going to believe in yourself? To trust yourself?"

"I'm trying." But I'm not sure if I really am or if I'm just pretending to. And him, I'm still confused about something he said. "You get it? How?"

Tegan drops his head into his hands, rubbing his face. He's been there for me so many times, in so many ways, that I just want to do the same for him, so I grab his hand. "What is it?"

"You know how I said I hate pity?"

I nod my head.

"It's such bullshit, because on the one hand I hate it, but on the other... I pity myself."

There is so much pain...so much regret in his voice, that it tears me up inside. "Why?"

"Not now," he tries to smile. "You know," Tegan looks down at me, still holding me tight. "It's been way too long since I kissed you. Wanna sneak into the bushes and make-out?"

Again, I let him change the subject. "How old are you? I swear, sometimes I think Tim is more mature than you."

"But I make you smile. It's a pretty smile. You should totally do it more often and you should totally kiss me before I pull your hair, or chase you or something. That's what little boys like me do when they like a girl, right?"

I shake my head. "You're a nerd."

He leans closer. "Will the third time be the charm?"

I don't have it in me to make him ask again. I let my mouth find his. My tongue sneaks out, needing to taste Tegan. It's so familiar, the way we move together now. The way I sense his movements and give when he wants to take, and take what he offers to me. His hand slides down, down until he's touching my rear. *Oh my God!* I'm all sorts of dizzy, feeling little sparks igniting inside me. When his hand slides up again, I'm scared he will pull away, but instead his hand slides under the back of my shirt. We're skin to skin, his rough fingers somehow smooth as they drift up and down my back.

I want to take him in. Every part of him. And I want to touch him too, so I do, testing the waters by letting my hand drift beneath his shirt. He's hard where I'm soft. Firm where I'm not, but right now, all I can do is revel in the differences because they make him, him and me, me. These moments, when he's moaning into my mouth and obviously as lost to sensation as I am, that's all that matters. Tegan being Tegan and me being me. Together.

"We're going to get in trouble for indecent exposure if we don't stop," he says against my mouth. "As good as you feel, we have to stop. I'm game with picking up where we left off later tonight."

I groan. "We have to?"

242

"Pick up later?"

"No, stop."

"Yeah. If I'm going to meet your parents, which I totally am, you know. I've wanted to anyway and now Mommy Dearest gave me a reason. But if we want them to like me, I probably shouldn't get us arrested from going at it in public." He offers his signature wink.

Going at it? Little firecrackers pop in my belly, but then I realize what he said. "You'd really suffer through a meeting with my mom for me?"

"Annabel Lee, when are you going to realize there's not much of anything I wouldn't do when it comes to you?"

***

My leg won't stop bouncing up and down. I seem to have completely lost control over it. Even though I haven't eaten all day, I'm not hungry. Tegan will be pissed if he finds out I skipped meals, but honestly, the thought of food makes me want to hurl. I've texted Tegan a million times to make sure he doesn't want to back out. It wouldn't hurt my feelings, I explained. I would understand. He started off humoring me by telling me he couldn't wait (which, hello? Has to be a lie. Why would someone be excited to torture themselves with my family?), but by the end I only get replies like, 'shut up' and 'I'm ignoring you now'.

He has no idea what he's getting himself into. Mom is rough around the edges under normal circumstances. Add in the fact that we've hardly spoken since I dropped the bomb about having a boyfriend she never thought I could get and I'm a little nervous about sending him into enemy territory without any ammo.

All of this isn't the only thing making my leg jump up and down like it's on crack. No. My first boyfriend, the boy I'm pretty sure has kidnapped my heart is coming to meet my parents. He's doing it for me. Because he wants to help, because he wants to know everything about me. That's enough to make a girl go crazy on its own.

Dad comes around the corner and into the entry way that's become my home for the past fifteen minutes just as the doorbell rings. I jump, fidgeting with my hands.

"Relax, pumpkin. You're not going up against a firing squad here."

Funny he seems to subconsciously realize Tegan and I will be under fire too.

"I don't know what's wrong with me."

"You'll be fine." He slides his hand down the side of my head and kisses my temple. "I'm the one who should be freaking out here. My little girl is bringing a boy home. In some ways, it's every father's worst nightmare, but you know what? I figure I'm pretty lucky because my little girl is an incredible young lady with a good head on her shoulders. If she likes a guy enough to bring him home, I know he has to be pretty special."

I blink to hold back tears. "I love you, Daddy, and he is. He's almost as special as you."

The bell rings again. "Go on. Answer the door and stop trying to suck up." His voice cracks and I know he realizes what I'm saying.

Shaking my hands as though I can make all the nervous energy fall out of me, I step forward and open the door. And I can hear it now, the scoffs people would let loose if they heard my thoughts because two months ago, I would have done the same thing. But seeing him there—Tegan with his blond waves, his electric smile and those eyes that always see more than I want to show —makes me forget to be nervous.

The way he steps toward me, kissing the opposite temple than my father just did, but in a completely different way. The way his hand lingers on my waist. It all makes me feel like I can face any army, any enemy as long as he's by my side.

"We ready for this?" he whispers into my hair.

"We're ready for anything."

One quick squeeze to my waist and a kiss to my hair later, he steps away from me, holding his hand out for Dad. "Hey, Mr. Conway. I'm Tegan. It's great to finally meet you."

Chapter Nineteen

WITH YOU I CAN WIN ANY WAR

"So, Tegan. Annabel hasn't taken the time to tell us how the two of you met?"

I tense at Mom's statement. That's such a lie. I told her about the gym and him being my trainer. It's just her way to make it seem like I'm keeping stuff about him from her. And the way she says his name? It's worse than how she says Em's.

Tegan's sitting beside me. Close to me—having moved the chair over. He finishes chewing, sets his fork down and replies. "I started out as her trainer at the gym. We kind of hit it off from the beginning."

I can't help it, I chuckle. What world is he living in?

"Okay, well maybe that's a stretch. The first day, I'm pretty sure she wanted me to die a fiery death."

I love that he's being himself. He's polite and respectful to them, but he's also not tempering down his sense of humor...or his ego. It's that take it or leave it attitude I wonder if I'll ever have. "I didn't want you to die..."

"I'm pretty sure you wanted me to die, Annabel Lee. I felt the daggers every time you looked at me."

"Hey! That's not fair. I wasn't *that* bad. I just didn't—"

"Like me?"

Giving him a smile, I tease, "Shut up."

When Mom clears her throat, I realize we kind of forgot they were here.

Tegan looks back and forth between my parents. "So yeah, we started working out together and things just took off from there. She and my mom got close. I'm pretty sure my brother likes her more than he does me, but that's because she's great with him. Treats him like he's a real person, ya know?"

"Actually, I don't. Annabel, you didn't tell me you've met his family."

Dad cuts in before I can reply. "Do you mind if I ask about your brother, Tegan? Annabel didn't mention anything so I didn't realize…"

"No problem. He's paralyzed," is all he says about Tim. Then he looks at Mom again. "She's doing awesome, you know. Not that I care or anything. I don't mean it like that, but she's amazing. Working real hard." It's one of the first times I've seen him stumble over his words and it sort of makes me love him even more.

"That's very nice of you to say, Tegan." Dad gives me a wink.

"And you live where? Close by here? How old are you? I wasn't aware teens could be trainers." Mom's interrogation continues, sneakily trying to figure out if he passes the Hillcrest elite test.

"I live down in the older part of town. Mom, my brother and I share an apartment over there. She's a waitress a few miles from our place. I graduated this past June and I'm eighteen. Turn nineteen a few days after Annabel's birthday."

In a few weeks. We've already planned to celebrate our birthdays together.

"Well, that's a pretty ambitious job for someone your age. Most kids are working at the mall." What she's saying sounds all nice and dandy, but I know what she's doing. She's looking for information. Whatever she can find to build a case.

"Mom..."

"It's cool," Tegan tells me. "I've always liked being physical. I'm considering a career that has to do with the human body so I figured it would be a great place for me to start. It only took a few classes. Plus, I'm saving for school too." No shame. No fear. No bringing up doing it for Tim, which I know he does because he doesn't want the pity. Just honesty.

Dad jumps in. "That's very respectable. It sounds like you have a good head on your shoulders, son. I'm not sure if Annabel told you, but I'm an orthopedic doctor. If you ever want to talk bones or the body, I'm always up for it." Dad's voice sounds way too excited. It's endearing, but I'm also not sure I want my boyfriend hanging out with my dad. "Annabel wants to go into medicine too." He adds with pride.

"She told me. I bet you love that she's following in your footsteps."

"I do. That's my pumpkin—"

"Daniel," Mom warns him. Then all her attention is on Tegan again. "I have to say, we were pretty surprised to hear about you. And then the...unconventional way you met. Annabel's always had such a good head on her shoulders."

My whole body freezes. I open my mouth to speak, but Tegan cuts me off. "With all due respect, I'm not sure how her dating me means she doesn't have a good head on her shoulders."

Mom waves him off. "That's not what I meant. The lying. The sneaking around, like she has something to hide. She didn't even tell us she finally decided to try and lose weight. I have to wonder where it's all coming from."

Ready. Aim. Fire. I knew this would come. Knew she couldn't stand to see me happy. What I don't understand is why. "Mom—"

"Well, like you said, Annabel's a smart girl. She knows what she's doing so if she decided to keep things from you, I can only assume she had a good reason to. And just so you know, she's not *trying* to lose weight, she has. She is. That's if you care enough to wonder." Tegan shrugs.

Mom's eyes turn to ice. "I don't appreciate the way you're talking to me in my own home. About my own daughter. Of course I care about her. What I have to wonder is…do you? You've already admitted to needing money. Is that why you latched onto her? Because you knew she had money and knew she would fall for it?"

"Paulette!"

I don't let Dad finish. "I don't appreciate the way *you're* talking to my boyfriend! It's obvious you think I'm too weak-minded to realize if someone is using me or not, and I've always known you don't think I'm good enough for someone to actually like me the way I am—" I'm so mad, I don't have it in me to cry right now. I feel like I could explode.

"That's not what I meant, Annabel. I'm trying to—"

251

"No, it *is* what you meant and I'm used to it. I don't care, but it's not fair to him! He's done nothing but care about me. No matter what he's there for me and for you to accuse him of using me for money? I knew you hated me, but." Now the tears are coming. I hate them, want to fight them so I don't give her the pleasure.

"Annabel that's not..." Only she can't finish. She's looking at me, her eyes pleading me for something, but I can't give her anything. Not right now.

"I love Tegan and I can never forgive you for even thinking that about him. I'm done. We're out of here."

Tegan stands too. "Annabel Lee, maybe you should—"

"No. I'm not staying. I'm not talking." I look at Dad and he gives me a small nod. Without another word, Tegan takes my hand and we walk out. A couple minutes later we're in his car, driving away. Neither of us talk. I don't trust my voice. If it's even half as broken as my heart, I know nothing that comes out will make any sense. I relive her words over and over and hear what she's really saying. That I'm not good enough. Why would any good looking boy like me?

Tegan's driving fast. It only takes us about fifteen minutes to get to his house. I shake my head. "I can't be around anyone else right now."

252

"I know. They're gone for the night. Timmy had an out of town appointment with a specialist. They're staying at a hotel."

As if there aren't enough emotions swirling inside me, I'm suddenly hit with more. "I am so sorry! You should have told me. We could have done this another night. I mean, not that it went well, but you shouldn't have missed Tim's appointment to have dinner with my family. I know you like to go."

He reaches out and cups my cheek. "Hey, don't do that. Not right now. I told you, I wanted to have dinner with your parents. I go to most of Timmy's appointments. It's not going to hurt me to miss one."

Words escape me. I'm not as good at them as he is. It's always so much harder for me to find the right thing to say. Because this... this is big. He did this for me. Buying time, I look around us. We're in his garage. How did I not realize we were already parked in his garage? "Thank you. For everything, I mean."

"You don't have to thank me for anything. You're...being with you is the first thing I've done for me in a long time. We're a team. When are you going to realize that?"

His words are the air I breathe. The fluid that hydrates me. The food that nourishes me. They're everything, giving me everything I need.

He takes a few breaths. "Your mom? That sucks. I do think she was trying to protect you, in her own screwed up way."

I shake my head and look at my lap. "I wish. I've never been what she wants, but...I don't want to talk about her right now. I just want to forget that dinner ever happened."

Tegan's finger slides beneath my chin and he turns my head so it's facing him. "I'm not sure I can forget it, Annabel Lee. I learned something pretty damn crucial tonight."

In my mind, I try and replay our evening. Try and figure out what he possibly could have learned that's so important.

He takes a deep breath. "I can see the wheels working. Should I put you out of your misery and tell you what it is? Or...I can always hold the information as ransom. You know, to get what I want out of you."

"If you don't tell me, I might have to introduce you to my hook again."

Tegan leans forward. "No, I don't want my ass kicked again, so I'll tell you." Closer still, he's leaning across the seat. "I found out you feel the same way as I do."

"Huh?"

"You love me…" My eyes widen as I look at him. How could I have forgotten? I'd told my parents I love Tegan and he'd been sitting right *there*. I admitted it to him and now here he is saying…

"I love you too, Annabel Lee."

Tingling excitement builds in my belly, exploding in every direction like the final fireworks display on Fourth of July. It reaches every piece of me from the tip of my head to my toes. There has to be a cheesy smile on my face that probably touches each of my ears, but I don't care because this is Tegan and I can be cheesy and dorky around him and he'll still…love me.

"I take it this is good news?" With his thumb, he traces my lips. I giggle. Yes, giggle. I don't care either.

"That's part of it right there. I love your laugh. Love how you make me feel good. You make me want to find the good in everything. Make me realize there are good people out there. People who will always stick by your side."

Swoon! "I love you." It feels good to say it. *Right* to say it.

"I love you too." His fingers slide from my face and into my hair. "How about we go inside? We can eat since dinner got screwed up. Watch a movie or something. Just hang out. Forget about everything else." Tegan leans forward. Now it's his mouth instead of his fingers tracing my lips. "Make out."

I force myself to pull away. "What are we waiting for?"

Chapter Twenty

SECRETS AND LOVE

Before we do anything, I text Dad, tell him I'll be home tomorrow and tell him not to worry. I know he won't be *happy,* but I think he'll understand. Okay, maybe understand isn't the right word, but he'll see why I can't be home with her tonight. Or maybe I'm delusional, which is why I turn my phone off so I won't get any texts demanding me to come home. This way, I don't have to directly disobey an order. It's not my fault my battery died. Or so my excuse will go.

We throw a quick dinner together, interrupted only by a slight food fight that I swear I didn't start. The mustard accidentally flew off the butter knife and hit him. Totally not my fault, but I'm still a little miffed Tegan got to be the one to end it. Stupid boys.

"I'm a mess and I have no clothes to wear." It looks like you could make a sandwich out of my shirt there's so much mustard and mayonnaise on it. Food isn't a real flattering look, by the way.

"Come on. I'll get you one of my shirts."

I follow Tegan to his room. He pulls a plain white t-shirt out of his drawer and tosses it at me. Instantly I wonder if it will smell like him. Like his ocean and soap, but I don't want to look like a weirdo by taking a sniff.

"You can change in here. I'll go clean up your mess."

"My mess?"

"Yep," he teases and then he's gone, leaving the door open behind him.

I stare at the opening and wonder if I should close it. There's no one here except the two of us and he knows I'm changing so he probably won't come back in. That's when it hits me. I wouldn't care if he came back in. If he saw me in a way no other boy had before. Actually, I want him to. You'd think that realization would surprise me, but it doesn't. It's already nuzzled up inside me and taken residence there. This need to share something with him, to see a part of him and show him a part of me.

Gah! I've totally turned into a horny teenage boy!

Rolling my eyes, I pull my shirt over my head and slide his on. It's tight over my chest, which is embarrassing. I look like I might burst out of it, but I'm surrounded in his scent, in something that's his, so that's what I try and focus on.

"Kitchen's clean. I need to change my shirt too real quick and I'll wash them both." He has his back to me as he grabs another shirt out of his drawer. He rips off the dirty one and tosses it in the basket next to him. My breath hitches. I'd forgotten what he looks like without a shirt. All tight, golden skin. The tattoo on his arm. The way his shorts aren't *overly* baggy, but enough that I still get to see his strip of boxers.

"Toss your shirt in the basket," he's turning as he talks to me. A smile tilts half his mouth. "Are you checking me out, Annabel Lee?"

After all this time, I shouldn't, but I blush.

Tegan walks over to me. "You can look all you want, ya know? Look or don't look. It's all up to you, but I can say, if the situation were reversed, I'd definitely want to explore every part of you."

A baseball slides down my throat. I want. Believe me, I totally want, but all of a sudden, those pesky nerves shove their way in. I'm scared if I do touch, I won't want to stop and I need to warm myself up to the idea a little more. "I want to…to know every part of you too, but maybe…I'm sorry—"

259

He quiets me with his mouth. It's not the kind of kiss I'm used to from him. There's no tongue. No open mouths tasting each other, just a quick, hard push of his lips against mine. "Shh, no excuses, no apologies and no pressure." He pulls the shirt over his head and I instantly miss the sight. "Now come on. I need you to show me how to work the washer."

It's an excuse and I know it. I've seen the way Tegan and his family are together and there's no way this boy doesn't wash his own clothes, but I'm glad for the distraction.

We start the laundry and then eat our soup and sandwiches. Tegan grabs a set of cards and I beat him two out of three games of Rummy. He pretends to be all surly about it and I pretend to gloat.

"Wanna watch a movie?"

I tell him yes as we sit on his couch. Tegan grabs the remote and we go through the movies and buy one of the new release comedies.

"What are you doing way over there?" Tegan pats the couch beside him and I close the two feet we'd had between us. When he puts an arm around me, I nuzzle against him. "That's better."

I giggle. Stupid, giggle.

It's hard for me to pay much attention to the movie. I laugh at a few places, but not as many as he does. I can't stop focusing on the way his fingers are drawing circles on my arm. The way he holds me like he wants nothing more than for me to be next to him. I still can't believe it. Out of all the girls he could have. Girls like Pammie, he's chosen me to hold. Me to watch a movie with, to jog with, to kiss and talk to. It's me he says he loves. The first and only guy I've ever loved loves me too. How did I get here?

I'm so lost in thought. So lost in Tegan that I don't realize the credits are rolling until he talks to me.

"You're quiet over there. Are you thinking about your mom?"

Ugh, I wasn't, but now I hear all her words again. All the comments she's made to me over the years. The way I'm good enough for Tegan, but not for her. "I would have done anything to make her happy. For her to like who I am, but now…it's like I realize it'll probably never happen."

"Hey. No." He turns and so do I. We're looking at each other now. "She loves you. That stuff she said to me? That's because she wants to make sure I'm not screwing around with you. I just, I don't know. I don't think she really knows how to talk to you, or something, but don't think you're not good enough. And don't ever think she feels that either."

Everything inside me perks up at his words. They're comforting even though I'm not sure they're true. "She likes things perfect. I'm not perfect."

"Who the fuck is? I know I'm not. All we can do is the best we can. You're incredible, Annabel Lee. The way you are with Timmy. The basketball with him and the card games. The way you keep me around even though I don't tell you nearly the things you tell me. It's impossible to know you and not see how incredible you are."

He's wrong. He *is* perfect. It's on the tip of my tongue to tell him, but he speaks before I can. "You should talk to her. Really talk to her. Tell her how you feel and let her be real with you. I'll bet you guys will figure out you have more in common than you think. And if you don't, screw it. You did what you could so it's all on her."

"No way. I can't talk to her. There's *no* talking to my mom, Tegan. She only sees what she wants. Plus, I'm so mad at her right now, I don't think I ever want to talk to her again."

Smiling at me, he shakes his head. "Well for the record, I'm on team talk to your mom. You've come so far, baby. I think your last roadblock is her."

And she'll steamroll me right to the ground. I know that. "I don't want to talk about her."

He looks at his cell phone. "It's getting late. Want me to take you home?"

I don't want to go home. I want him. I love him and everything inside me wants to take that next step. Not to show him I love him because I think we've both shown each other how we feel. We both *know* how we feel, but I want something physical. Another thing that's only ours. "I texted my dad and told him I'm not going home tonight."

Suddenly, it's Tegan who looks nervous. He bites his lip, his eyes huge pools of brown that are on me. "I get you all night?" You can hear how he tries for light, but the way his voice cracks, the truth breaks through. He's just as nervous as I am. Has he done this before?

"Yeah. If you want to bring me home, I understand. I just…"

"I want you here, Annabel. You have to know that." Without another word, he stands up, turns off the TV and makes sure his front door is locked. Walking back over to me, he holds out his hand. I take it, locking our fingers together as we head back to his room. This time, he closes the door behind us, locking it. It's so strange how you can be scared to death, but completely excited. How you can know you want something more than anything else in the world, know how right it is for yourself, but you're still freaked out you're going to screw it up.

"No pressure," he says, reading my mind. My heart is seriously beating faster than it ever has, but somehow, when his lips touch mine, its soothing, like a melody my heart is so in tune to, it slows to match the beat.

Our mouths match up perfectly, our tongues dance to mine and Tegan's music. I know his taste and wonder if mine is as familiar to him. I've memorized the feel of his hands in my hair like they are now. The way he runs his fingers through the strands when he deepens our kisses. It's so us. So natural the way I always feel with him. Like it's been carved in the walls of caves millions of years ago, made out in the stars, this moment is destiny. It's meant to be.

Pulling away, Tegan grabs my hand again and leads me over to the bed. When I sit down, he kneels in front of me, sliding one of my ballet flats off, then the other one.

"We can lie in this bed and hold each other all night, if that's what you want. I don't expect anything."

"I know." Looking down at him, I continue. "Have you done this before?" I'm not sure why I want to know.

"Yeah. One other girl. But it's not the same. Nothing feels like we do together. No one feels like you." And for the first time ever, Tegan blushes.

"I haven't. I'm sure you knew that, but yeah, I haven't." With only the slightest fear, fear so small it's eclipsed by the way I know how right this is, I say. "But I want to. With you. No one feels like you either."

He gives me a vulnerable smile. No teasing, no cockiness. Just a boy. Just Tegan.

"Do you have protection?"

He nods yes, then stands, pulling a foil package out of his wallet and setting it on the bedside table. Next he pulls his shirt off and it lands on the floor. His shorts come off next, kicked into a pile with his shirt. He's wearing nothing but his boxers, and he's beautiful. I find my way to my feet, my hands touch his stomach, his chest, his shoulders, his back. I'm exploring him the way he said I could. The warmth of his skin singes my fingers in the most delicious way.

"Can I?" His hands are at the bottom of my shirt, and they're shaking gently.

Unable to find words, I nod. Tegan pulls his shirt over my head. I'm in my bra. In my bra in front of a boy and there's no embarrassment because it's him and he loves me and I can do anything with Tegan by my side.

With those same shaky fingers, he pushes the button through its hole, slides down my zipper and my pants are gone too. Now his fingers touch me, my thighs, my stomach, and it feels so good. Like nothing I've ever felt. Like each touch is a vibration flooding out so I feel him everywhere. The brush of his fingers is like a feather tickling me from head to toe. The epicenter of an earthquake. Wherever he touches me is that epicenter, but the aftershocks, the vibrations can be felt everywhere else in my body.

"I want to lie down with you," he says against my ear, kissing me there. He leads me into his bed. "Are you sure?"

"Yes."

"Are you scared?"

"A little."

"You're beautiful."

"So are you."

Tegan settles on top of me, taking my mouth. He removes my bra and panties. I take off his boxers. There's more touching, him on me and me on him. We're both on an adventure to discover a new land. After so much touching I think I'm going to unravel, he opens the foil package. When we're protected, he's above me again. Our mouths come together and then our bodies, meet in the same way: exploring depths, dancing in unison to a tune that's only ours.

Finally, we both really do unravel, and we do it together.

***

"Can I tell you a secret?"

"You can tell me anything."

"I know." But then he doesn't. He's quiet for what feels like a lifetime.

"I'm... I'm mad at Timmy." I've thought I heard pain in Tegan's voice before. Thought I heard heartbreak, tenseness, but those times were nothing compared to the statement he just made. It's like he had to rip each word` out, breaking a part of him in the process.

"Tegan, you're too hard on yourself. You would do anything for your brother." Ugh. What a lame thing to say, but he caught me by surprise and I'm lost—lost on how to help him through whatever it is he's dealing with.

"I would. Anything. I'd take his place if I could and, hell, I don't know. Maybe mad isn't the right word, it's just..." His arm wraps tighter around me. "We had everything, Annabel Lee. I was always running around, having fun, playing sports, getting into trouble. Timmy was only eleven, but loved football. He could throw a ball better than people my age. We were always out practicing, playing together. My parents—they were happy. So happy. We all were."

Tiny drops of water roll off his face and onto me. Tegan. The strong, responsible boy who can handle anything is crying and there's nothing I can do. I want to make it better for him like he's done for me. Take his pain the way he would take Tim's paralysis. But I can't. All I can do is listen.

"I didn't even want to fucking play that day, but I went. One hit. One screwed up hit was all it took, Annabel. How does that even happen? How can your body break that easily?"

"I don't know." I wish I did. Wish Tegan and his family never had to deal with this.

My tears are now mixing with his. Every part of us has come together now.

"You know what? It's not Timmy I'm upset with, it's just the whole thing. One minute we have everything and then we're the family with the crippled brother and the dad who ran out on them. How could he do that?"

Tegan's voice cracks, the sound shattering me into a million different pieces. I kiss his hair, his cheek, his chest. It's so small, such a nothing thing to do, but it's all I have.

"I *hate* him. I use to look up to him, but I will *never* let myself be the kind of man he is." Tegan seethes. "What kind of person walks away from their family like that? When it gets hard, who just bails like that?"

It's then I know the answers to all the questions I've wondered about Tegan. "That's why you do it, isn't it? That's why you work so hard. Why you try to be there for everything with Timmy, help your mom. Your trying to make up for him, aren't you?"

I thought I loved him before. Thought I knew what it meant to love someone—to know someone, but at this moment, everything I knew then is so small compared to what I know—how I feel about him now.

"I needed to know that people don't just walk away... I needed to prove it, to them and to me. That I could be the person he wasn't—the one they deserved. Who would take care of responsibilities no matter how hard it is because that's what you do when you love someone. It's the right thing to do."

"You're incredible."

He shakes his head. "Not really because I'm pissed too. So mad that Dad is out there doing whatever the hell he wants while I'm working like crazy. I'm so pissed about everything that was taken from me. How shitty is that? Timmy is in a wheelchair, but I think about what I've missed."

Could he take on any more responsibility? "Anyone would feel like that. What matters is you're doing it. You're doing it because you love them."

Tegan rolls over so he faces me. His finger slides down the side of my face when he speaks. "That first day, when you helped? Part of me was mad because it was such a small thing to do, helping with the chair, but you did it. Not knowing us you did it, but our own dad took off? You hung out with Mom and Timmy, played basketball with them. Had fun. You wanted to be there, but our dad doesn't?"

Leaning forward, I kiss him, just because I can't *not* do it.

"Want to know another secret?" he asks.

"I want to know anything you want to tell me."

He tries to smile at me, but it doesn't reach his eyes. "I don't know if I really want to be a physical therapist. I mean, I think I do. I enjoy what I do now even though it's different. The body really is amazing to me. The things it can do and how it works. I think it's what I want, but I don't know. I can't say for sure and it scares the hell out of me that I'm going to do it, that I'll sign up for it and realize it's not what I want for my life, but how can I not? How can I not try and fix Timmy? It's like… like it feels like that's walking away from him just like our dad did."

"Oh, Tegan, no one expects you to try and fix it. You can't change it and I know your mom or Tim wouldn't want you to jump into something you don't want."

He gives me another smile before pulling my head down so it rests against his bare chest. "The only thing I'm sure about is you. When I'm with you, it's the only time I feel like I can just, *be*. It's the only time I don't want all the pressure on me."

I start to cry again, because as much as I hate to see him hurt, it feels good to know I do something for him. That after everything he's done, I somehow have a way to give him something back. "You're wrong, you know. Earlier you said no one's perfect. I'm pretty sure you are."

His chest vibrates against my cheek when he laughs. "No, but thanks for inflating my ego again. I needed it. I can't believe I *cried* in front of you."

I trace the muscles in his chest and stomach, trying not to let him just push this aside, to forget himself like he always does. "I mean it, Tegan. No one wants you to try and make up for something that wasn't your fault. They love you. I love you. Ahh!"

He flips me over so he's on top of me again. "I love you, too." Then with a mischievous smile that is so him, "Want to do it again?"

Chapter Twenty-One

OPPOSITES

Did u talk to ur mom? Is she pissed at you?

My lips automatically stretch into a smile as I read Tegan's text. Even though it's 10:00 PM, the night *after* I lost my virginity to Tegan and we spent the whole day together, I've only been home about forty-five minutes and he's already texting.

No, didn't talk. She told me to nver stay out overnight again, but that's all. I hit reply.

Sorry. Don't want u in trouble. Don't want u to fight over me.

I'm not in trouble and we nver get along. No big.

I miss you.

My heart starts to pitter-patter. **I miss you too.**

I love u.

I love u, too.

Nice. Ferris Buhler's on. Old school, but love it.

I've never watched it. I text back.

What? It's one of my favs. Watch it with me?

I want to, so bad, but I know I can't leave again. My parents definitely wouldn't let me get away with it twice. **Can't leave** ☹

I know. Turn it on. Channel 58.

Suddenly, I get all giddy. It's a dumb thing to get excited about after everything that's happened, but hey, I never claimed I'd be good at all this stuff. For me, wanting to watch a movie with me, while we're texting ranks pretty high on the sweetness scale. I pick up my remote, turn it on, and settle into my bed. It's on.

Are u in ur room?

Yeah.

Damn. Can't get a visual cuz I've never seen it.

With shaky fingers I text him a brief description of my room.

Thx. I'm on the couch, in the living room.

Okay. Oh, Matthew Broderick. Forgot he's in this.

Shh. I like this part ;)

I can't help it, I smile. We finish watching our movie together, Tegan texting me during all his favorite parts. LOL-ing when he laughs. All too soon the movie is over.

Going to bed. Meet me in AM to jog?

Absolutely.

Love u, Annabel Lee.

I love u too.

***

Tegan's there when I step out of the car the next morning. "Hey, you." I'm tentative when I step toward him, waiting for the insecurities to hit, the nerves or something. Waiting to see how he'll react. It's a big deal to see the person you had sex with for the first time afterward. A defining moment, I think. Are there any regrets? Do we feel weird? Did it change anything? Add in our talk from that night and it makes it an even bigger deal.

"Hey. You look nice. Did you put make-up on to run?" He locks his hands around my waist and pulls me toward him. My eyes automatically cast downward and Tegan chuckles. "Annabel, you don't have to try and impress me."

"I know. It's lame. I just…" Have no idea how to explain without looking like a moron. Why did I put make up on? This boy has seen me with no layers, seen me laid bare in a way no one else ever has. And I've seen him the same way. "I have no idea what I was thinking."

"You were probably distracted by pure excitement at the thought of seeing me. I get it. I seem to have that affect— ouch. Don't pinch me. Why are you always beating me up?"

"You will never change. Not that I want you to. Ever. I should have known I can always be comfortable with you. That I don't need to try so hard."

275

"You don't have to try at all." He pushes my hair behind my ear. "I know who you are and you're who I want." His lips capture mine. It's different and the same, kissing him afterward. I like it even more.

A few seconds later, I break the kiss. "Come on. Run with me."

"Slave driver," he teases, already starting to jog. Easily, I fall in line with him, keeping pace. Maybe even setting it.

***

Tegan hasn't texted me for two days. Let me rephrase that, he's replied to my texts, one or two word answers, he's even told me he loves me the couple times we actually spoke on the phone, but he hasn't called first. He hasn't texted first.

For the first time since the beginning, there's a weight in my stomach when I pull up at Let's Get Physical. It's fighting to hold me down, to pull me under. The harder I try and swim to shore, the more I tell myself I'm imagining things, that nothing's different. He's just busy like he says, the heavier the weight becomes, the harder I have to fight.

I'm a worrier, right? Always waiting for the other shoe to drop—which is about the dumbest saying in the world, if you ask me, but that has to be what this is. Tegan wouldn't be pulling away. It's not him. Unlike me, he's not a runner.

I turn off the engine to see him waiting for me out front, like always. See? Everything's okay, I try and tell myself. He pushes off the wall and comes toward me.

"Hey."

"Hey, Annabel Lee. I missed you."

The weight starts to lose its pull. "I missed you too. Is everything okay?"

He tries to smile. I physically *see* how much effort he puts into it, but it's not the same smile I know. It's not Tegan. "It's better now."

As he pulls me toward him, and kisses me, all I think is no, it's not better. Something's wrong that he doesn't want to share with me.

***

Tegan's arms are shaking as he pushes the weight bar up again. It's more weight than he usually lifts. More repetitions than he usually does. Each push of the bar, puts a crack in my heart. Something's off. I feel it in the nausea churning in my gut. See it in fierceness of Tegan's workout.

"That's twelve. That's enough, right?"

"Two more," he pushes up again, and that's when it happens. He grunts. Now, I know that's a ridiculous thing to let bother me, but it does. It echoes through the room until that's all I hear, because it's not Tegan's style. As much as he likes to pretend to be cocky, he's not a showoff. He doesn't try and out-lift everyone in the gym, grunting his way to the top by pushing more weight than he can handle. I bite my lip, then jump when the bar clanks back into its spot.

"Tegan." I touch his arm when he stands up, a little zip of electricity zapping from him to me. "What's wrong? You know you can tell me anything." And I can say anything to him, no fear.

He sighs, then drops his head forward. It takes him a few minutes before his eyes raise to mine again. "Shit. I'm sorry."

"Don't be. Just tell me what's going on."

He grabs my hand and weaves through the workout machines and out the front door. Like always, my hand feels warm in his. Feels right and I know right now we're going to talk and everything's going to be better again. He leans against my car, which is parked right in front of the gym and then in that familiar way, he holds my waist and pulls me toward him. His body is tense and when he smiles, it's the Ken smile.

"I'm all screwed up right now."

I push myself closer to him, needing to feel him, all of him, tight against me. "Why? What can I do?"

"Nothing." He shakes his head. "I just...I just have to work it out, but I love you. Just bear with me and I'll figure it all out." For the first time, I worry he's lying to me. Maybe even lying to himself. His voice is off. And even though he might not know it, deep down inside, as deep as the marrow in my bones, I somehow know I'm going to lose him. How will I do this without him?

"I'm here. I'll do anything you need. I'll always be here for you."

He brushes my cheek with the back of his hand. "I love you. I'll work it out." It's everything I want, but not enough at the same time, but when his lips meet mine, I can't help but hope I'm wrong. That this is a little blip in time that means nothing. That things will magically get better by the way his tongue dips so needy, into my mouth.

"Holy shit! Annabel Conway? What the hell happened to you?"

I freeze against Tegan, but it's nothing compared to the way his body unnaturally stiffens. Pulling away from Tegan, I turn to see Billy and crew. I can't believe they're on this side of town.

"It is you." He elbows Patrick. "Dude, check it out. Annabel has a boyfriend."

"Who the hell are you?" Tegan steps away from me and toward Billy.

I see a light in Billy's eyes that tells me he's about to do something stupid. He knows he's untouchable. For some reason he likes hurting me. "Tegan, let's go."

"Is this him?" He looks at me and I know he knows this is Billy.

"Let's go back inside."

"Yeah, go back inside, *Tegan.* You don't want to mess with me. I'm a friend of your girlfriend's." Then he looks at me and I want to puke. "Lookin' pretty good, Conway. Not quite there yet, but lookin' good. I never would have thought—"

Before I can stop him, Tegan is in front of Billy. "Walk away. Don't say another word to her, and walk away." There's a fierceness in Tegan's voice I've never heard before.

"Tegan. Come on, he's not worth it." I hope, pray he'll walk away. He locks eyes with me and takes a step away from Billy and toward me. That's when Billy swings, hitting Tegan in the jaw while he's not looking.

I scream when Tegan charges at him. His arms go around Billy's middle and they fall to the ground. Billy swings. I *hear* his fist connect with Tegan's jaw again. Tegan falls off of him, but recovers quickly, punching Billy in the stomach when he comes back at him.

My body is on adrenaline overload. Fear and worry colliding and crashing inside me. "Stop! Both of you stop! Do something," I yell at Patrick.

"What do you want me to do? I don't wanna get hit!"

Pain shoots through me when Tegan takes a punch to the gut. He counters it with a swing to Billy, hitting him in the nose, blood gushes everywhere.

"You prick! You made me bleed."

"Leave her alone, you hear me? Stay the hell away from her." There's pain in his voice and it doesn't sound physical. There's more going on here. This isn't just about Billy. Tegan turns to walk away again.

"Fuck you." Billy charges Tegan. They hit the ground again, Tegan kicking Billy off of him. It's then that the owner of Let's Get Physical, Jim comes out.

"What the hell is going on out here?" The man is huge. Probably two Tegan's and a Billy put together. I've seen him before, but not often. "Tegan! Are you fighting outside my gym?" Easily, he steps between them. "Are you on the clock?"

"No." Tegan spits and blood comes out of his mouth. Tears overflow my eyes.

"He works here? He's crazy. He attacked me. I'm going to sue the hell out of him and anyone else I can. You better believe I'm pressing charges." Despite being bloody, Billy looks so proud of himself, I have to fight down the bile that's built in my stomach.

"That's not true!" I yell, running over to them. "Tegan tried to walk away, but Billy attacked him!"

"That's not the way I remember it."

"Yeah, me either." Patrick agrees with Billy.

"Get the hell off my property," Jim seethes. "You too, Tegan. You have some nerve bringing this shit to my place."

"I work in an hour."

"No, you don't."

Tegan's eyes pop up, meeting Jim's head on. I see his chest rise and fall he's breathing so heavily. "Fine."

In the background, I see Patrick, pulling a laughing Billy away.

"We'll talk later." Without a glance at me, Tegan turns and stalks off. I start to run after him.

"Tegan! Wait."

He turns and looks at me and shakes his head. "I can't right now. I'm sorry. I just...I just need to be alone."

And then he's gone, a trail of blood splattering on the sidewalk behind him, like breadcrumbs. Alone. I've never felt so alone in my whole life.

Chapter Twenty-Two
ALONE

I've always known news travels fast in Hillcrest, but I didn't realize how fast until Mom comes home livid, the same night of Tegan and Billy's fight. I haven't let go of my cell phone all day, hoping, praying for a text or call from Tegan. I hope he isn't hurt badly. I can't stop wondering what I did wrong and if I somehow made him stop loving me.

"Annabel! We need to talk. Now!"

I push my empty bowl of ice cream aside, yep, ice cream. It's always been my comfort, until Tegan was. Today, I need a little comfort. "Why? We've never talked before so what's the point now?"

She gasps and I'm a little proud of myself. "I'm going to ignore that. Can you imagine my embarrassment when three of my friends called me today to let me know your hoodlum boyfriend attacked Betty's son?"

There's no point in trying to set her straight so I don't. "No, but I'm sure you'll tell me." I pick up my bowl and head back to the kitchen. Of course, Mom follows.

———

"I'm not sure when you decided it's okay to talk to me like this, but I can assure you, it's not. And I won't have you dating someone who's violent, Annabel. If he attacked a nice boy like Billy, he could turn that violence on you."

I sputter, dropping the bowl to the floor, ignoring the shatter of glass. "Tegan would *never* hurt me. He's not violent. Did you ever think for one minute to ask my side of the story? That maybe he was protecting me? That maybe Billy hasn't always been so nice to me? Ninety percent of teenage boys have probably been in a fight, Mom. It doesn't make them violent, women-abusing jerks."

"Your relationship with him is over and what on Earth would Billy do to you?"

I notice how she brings it up second. Her most important issue being Tegan, not the possibility Billy has ever done anything wrong to me. "Well, thank you for your opinion, but no. I love him and I'm not breaking up with him."

Mom's face pales. "Oh, Annabel. You don't love that boy."

Heat engulfs me. "Oh, really? I wasn't aware you know or care anything about how I feel."

It shocks me when she steps forward. "I'm only saying this because I don't want you to get hurt and he will hurt you, Annabel. You might think you love him, but it's just because he's the first boy to ever show you attention. You're breaking up with him. Hate me all you want, but I'm doing it to protect you."

Ugh. I'm so tired of crying. Tired of tears and pain. *Open your mouth,* I tell myself. *Tell her you're tired of her assuming no one will want because you're not perfect. That you're tired of not being good enough for her.* But I can't. I still can't and it makes me hate myself even more. "I'm used to being hurt by now, Mom. I'll take my chances." With that, I run up the stairs and into my room. Alone again.

***

The next morning, I pull up at our spot for my jog with Tegan. He's already there waiting for me, his arms crossed as he leans against his car. One look at him, the way his eyes are looking at the ground and not me, the way his shoulders are slumped over and I know. There's a huge part of me that wants to put the car in reverse and pull away. If I don't give him the chance to say it, it won't be true, right?

But I can't. I try and gather up any courage I can, the stuff that made me shove Pammie, the strength that helped me fall in love with him and use it to push myself out of the car. "Hi." We usually say hey, why did I say hi?

"Hi. Sorry about yesterday." There are too many apologies between us lately. It's not what we're about.

"It's okay." But it's not.

"No, it's not."

"You're right. I need to work on that, I guess." It's something else for me to add to the list. "My mom already found out. She freaked out. She wants me to break up with you." Did I really just say that?

Tegan's eyes close and he lets out a heavy breath. His hands are shoved deep into his pockets. Jean shorts. He's wearing jean shorts and not basketball shorts. He always runs in basketball shorts.

I fight to keep my feet firmly planted to the ground. "Just say it, Tegan."

He looks at me, something in his eyes I can't decipher. Looks like pain, but if it is, why is he doing this? "Maybe she's right…"

I knew it was coming, maybe even before the past couple days. This is what I expected, right? I never thought it would last. But still, pain pierces through my chest with such strength I want to fall over. It spreads over me, slowly taking over my body until it's all I feel. All I know.

"I mean, it's not you. Not us. I still love you, but…"

"But what?" *Please don't say it. Change your mind. Tell me I'm good enough. Tell me you want me forever. That I was wrong and we can last. That we will.*

"I lost my job. I know that's not your fault. It's mine, but it's just one more thing. I need that job for the money. To help Mom and for school. And Timmy. I missed his appointment. I never would have done that before, but I did. And they got in a wreck and I wasn't there."

"What? Oh my God. Are they okay?" Not Tim, not Dana.

"They're fine. It was minor, but still. *I wasn't there.*" He's pacing and rambling. I've never seen him so shook up before. I want to go to him, hug him and make it better, but my feet won't move.

"Mom was exhausted and I was laughing with you. She almost fell asleep and went off the road. They could have died or been hurt and I was making love to you. I should have *been* there. If I had been there, I would have been driving." He drops to the curb, hands buried in his hair, his knee bouncing up and down. "What would I have done if they got hurt? It's my job to take care of them, Annabel."

I'm pulled in so many different directions. I want to run and pretend this didn't happen. Hug him and tell him we can work it out. Yell at him to open his eyes and realize he's not a superhero, but I can't. I can't make myself do any of it.

"I'm so sorry... I..."

His head jerks up at me. "It's not your fault, it's mine. That's how it started with him too. Missing appointments. Not coming home. I can't... I just can't."

I kneel next to him, needing to be closer. "We can slow down. I know you need time." Something... anything not to lose him.

289

Tegan pulls away. And it hurts. I'm usually the one pulling away. He's always getting closer, always reeling me in, but now he's the one drifting and I don't think I can pull him ashore. "You deserve so much better than that, Annabel Lee. I just... I have to. It's... it's the right thing to do." He cups my cheek and I know I've lost him. Leaning forward he presses his lips to my forehead too quickly and then he's to his feet. Walking away.

And then I'm alone. Broken and not good enough still.

Chapter Twenty-Three

155.8

Why is it, it takes weeks, months to lose weight, but then multiple pounds find their way back on in the matter of days? Forget the part that I've been eating too much. That all the good eating habits I've learned in the past two months, I left in the park with Tegan. Forget that I haven't gone running. Haven't gone to the gym, and don't want to. Still, it's depressing that the pounds find me so quickly. It's really not fair. A broken heart, and gaining weight. What else am I going to have to deal with?

Not Mom because she hasn't tried to talk to me.

Not Tegan because he hasn't contacted me either. Well, unless you count the "Happy Birthday, Annabel Lee" text I've stared at over and over.

Not Dad. He gave up trying to talk to me two days ago, though I'm sure with today being my birthday, I'll have to face him sometime. I don't care how pathetic I am. That I'm in bed on my birthday because my life is such a mess. It is what it is. But still, I miss him. Miss him more than I thought I could miss someone.

A cry seizes me. I haven't cried since the first day. I don't know why it's coming out again, but I let it flow without trying to fight it. It's the only thing I seem to have control over. Rolling over, my back is to the door as I hug a pillow. Does he miss me too? Did he really love me? How is Timmy, Dana? Does she know?

My cries only pause when I feel the arm that wraps around me, the girl that curls up behind me. It only takes that quick pause for me to know who it is and I start to cry harder. There are no words while I let it out. We don't need words. But once my tears finally dry, she speaks anyway.

"I was jealous, Bell," Em whispers. "Jealous you had someone else when I didn't. Scared you would realize you didn't need me anymore. I'm a terrible friend and I'm so sorry."

"No," I roll over and face her. "You're not a terrible friend. People make mistakes. It all started because *I* wasn't honest with you." It feels so good to see her. To have her here. To not feel alone. "I missed you, Em."

"Me, too. I missed you so much. I don't want to fight about whose fault it was. I just want to forget it. I want to be best friends again."

"We never weren't best friends. We always will be."

She smiles at me. "I'm sorry you're hurt. Do you want to talk about it? About him? I never gave you the chance to tell me anything about him and I want to know."

For the first time in days, I smile too. The coolest part is I actually *feel* it as well. I start to talk. I start from the beginning. I tell her about my first day at the gym, how Tegan talked me into staying and about his family. Our awkward first workouts together, how he showed me how to box when I felt bad, hitting him, and my first weigh in.

She laughs in all the right places. Smiles in all the right places and I'm doing the same. We talk about when I started to fall for him, our first date, first kiss, the jogs in the park, his support, the party, saying I love you, and about being with him. I don't give her all the details, because they're ours. Something Tegan and I will always share.

It's amazing how good it feels to talk about him. How I realize that even though we're over, what we had was true. You can't fake that. I still love him and I really believe he loved me too.

"I'm sorry I didn't get to meet him. Even though he hurt you, he sounds like a good guy."

"Perfect," I start to say, but cut myself off. I realize now, he's not perfect. He was right about that all along and it's not fair that I ever tried to make him feel that way. No one's perfect. He has issues just like me. It sucks to come to this realization now. Showing his imperfections in the park that day about killed me, but now it beats more life into me. Tegan's not perfect. He's just a guy. A gorgeous, sweet, wonderful, guy, but just a guy all the same.

He has fears, insecurities and regrets. He hurt me more than anyone ever has, but he loved me better than anyone ever did, too. "He is a good guy," I finally say. "I miss him."

"I'm sorry." She snuggles closer to me. We're still lying in my bed. It's like old times. Where we talk into the night. Best friends.

"He told me I need to talk to Mom. Tell her how I feel." Has he ever told Tim or Dana how he feels? Opened up to them?

"He's right, Bell. I've always thought that. I mean, I think she's the Wicked Witch, but I do think she loves you. In her own, screwed up, crazy way."

I'm not sure I agree, so I change the subject. "What made you come?"

"Your dad. He called and said he thought you needed me, so I came. But I'm not changing the subject so easily. Are you going to talk to her?"

I know I need to talk to her. Need to talk to Dad too. I need to get out of this bed. Try and get on track. I wanted to lose weight before Tegan, so I should still want it after. It shouldn't hinge on him. But it does. "There are so many things I need to do, but it's hard. He always made me feel like I could do anything. It's so much easier with him."

Em sits up. "I don't want to fight with you and I love you, but that's bullshit. If you want it, you need to do it for you. No one else. When are you going to realize you can do anything?"

Her words are eerily familiar. Tegan said the same thing to me so many times. It's like two on one, only these two people are both on my side. Tegan and I may be over, but I know his words were true. Or maybe I just want them to be true.

Before I can keep thinking about it, Em continues. "What did Tegan do for you that you couldn't do for yourself?"

"He…" Gave me a meal plan, but I'm the one who followed it. He gave me a workout routine, but I'm the one who did it. With him, yes, but still, I was out there. He supported me, but I have Em or Dad who will do that for me. And maybe I can even do it for myself. He believed in me, something I want to do in myself. Something maybe I can learn to do for myself. "Well…"

There were so many things Tegan did for me. I will never be able to pay him back for them, but they were tools. Tools that would have meant nothing if *I* hadn't used them. What would they have meant without my sweat? My tears? My determination? How many times did he talk about how determined I was, but am I really? I've tried to be, but here I am, lying in bed for days, throwing away every tool he gave me, all the hard work I put in.

"That's what I thought."

I sit up in my bed and hug Em. "It's one thing to realize something and it's another to change it."

"And you will."

That little surge of excitement I felt when I lost weight returns. The stinging in my muscles, or my war wounds as Tegan would call them. How they hurt, but in a good way, because they showed my hard work. I remember jogs I took without Tegan and how they felt even better than the ones I took with him, except in a different way. All the things I did and how freakin' *good* they felt. How even though it took me three times, I made my way into Let's Get Physical. I'm going to make it again. I'm going to do this. "Yeah, I will." But first, I have to find a way to make it over my first hurdle.

Chapter Twenty-Four

154.0

For three days I've been perfectly on track with my eating plan. My portions small, healthy and low fat. It was a hard breakup, but I had to say goodbye to Ben and Jerry's for the second time. I've jogged every morning. In our park. It's scary as all get out. What if I see him? What if it breaks me? But you know what? This is where I like to run and even though we're over, it doesn't mean I have to find somewhere else to go. It doesn't have to be *our* spot anymore. It can be *my* spot.

Em even came with me once. Jogging so isn't her thing, but I realize something. It *is* my thing. Ever since Tegan and I started, I knew I enjoyed it, but now I know I love it. I missed it the week I spent cuddling Ben and Jerry.

I'm not going to feel sorry for myself anymore. I'm not running from life anymore either.

Raising my hand, I knock on Mom's office door. There should be nerves, but there aren't. Or maybe they're there, but my willpower is stronger than the nerves. I'm doing this and nothing will stop me.

"Come in," I hear Mom call out.

Her eyes flash with shock when she sees it's me, but quickly, she recovers. "It's been good to see you out of your room the past couple days."

She's sitting behind her huge cherry wood desk. Patterns and samples are laid out in front of her, everything lined up in neat little rows. Perfectly Mom.

Biting my lip, I pull a chair from the corner and sit across from her. "I was hurting."

She sighs. "I know it feels like this is the end of the world, but it's not. We all get our hearts broken by our first loves."

"Did you?" I never get stories from her. She's not the type who shares easily. I'm not sure why. It's another of her secrets.

"I'm sure you didn't come in here to talk about my teenage love life."

No, but maybe I'd like to hear about it anyway. A shaky breath escapes my lungs. *I can do this. I need to do this. I want to do this.* "I never told you people at school give me a hard time about my weight. Call me names, tease me. That kind of thing."

"Why?" She sets her pen down, giving me her full attention.

"Because of my weight—I said that."

"No, why? Why didn't you tell me?"

I shrug. "I didn't want to bother you. I was embarrassed. I was pretty sure you agreed with all the things they say to me."

"Now you're being ridiculous." She shakes her head.

"No, I'm being honest."

"Why would you think that, Annabel? You're my daughter. In fact, if you tell me who harassed you, I'll take care of it for you."

All business. All the time. *I can do this. I can do this.*

"I don't want you to take care of it for me. I'm learning to do that for myself. I want...I want you to love me. To support me. I want to be enough for you."

Her facial expressions, body language, nothing changes. "What? That's absurd. You know I love you, Annabel."

I sit forward, wanting her to know how serious I am. Needing her to see me and know how much I've hurt. "Maybe I should, but I don't."

She rustles papers on her desk. "I'm sorry you feel that way. I'm not sure what I can do to change it though. Your father and I give you everything you need. I've offered to take care of who harassed you in school, though now that you're losing weight, it probably won't be an issue. Things will get easier, the more you lose. You'll see. I know it's hard, but that's just the way the world works."

I'm not sure what I can do to change it though. I've offered to take care of who harassed you. Now that you're losing weight. That's just the way the world work.

I don't hear anything else she said. Those aren't answers. "You don't know what you can do? You can love me!"

"Lower your voice, Annabel. I'm your mother. Of course I love you."

I open my mouth to counter it, but she stops me. "Sit down. I'm going to tell you a story."

Call me crazy, but I do it.

"Both my parents came from very poor families. They worked hard to get what they have and they both understood how the world works. You get ahead by being strong. By being the best you can be. They taught me that too. When I was younger, and something tried to break me, I got tougher. That's what you need to do. You work hard. You become the best and that's how you show everyone in your life who never thought you would amount to anything."

Her words open my eyes in a way I didn't expect. Maybe she does love me. Maybe she doesn't. I'm not sure I'll ever know. She is who she is and I'm who I am. Neither of us will change and there's nothing I can do about it.

Sometimes, that's life, I think. We don't always get the answers we need or want. Sometimes there aren't any. I don't like it, and I never will, but I'm not going to let her get me down.

Holding back my tears, I stand up. "You're right, Mom. You are tough and if being tough means I have to be like you...well, I'm not sure I'll ever be. We're always going to be different. I see that now."

With my head held high, I turn and walk out of the office. It's not what I wanted. What I expected, but I still jumped the hurdle and I did it on my own.

Chapter Twenty-Five
150.0

I'm now working out with the Hillcrest Elite. Well, not *with them*, with them, but at the same gym. I've seen Mom here over the past two weeks, some of her friends, Elizabeth and a few of the other girls from school. Beforehand, I would have thought I'd feel uncomfortable, like I don't fit with them. While I don't fit in some ways they're just the kind of things that make people different—not something that makes one person better than the other. You know, diversity makes the world go round and all that stuff.

I'm keeping the routine Tegan taught me, except I'm taking a class here and there. So far I've tried Step Aerobics and Cycling. Can I just say that cycling is no joke? I thought my butt was going to fall off it burned so bad, but it's another war wound I'm glad I have. Cycling is my new goal. Soon, maybe in a week, a month, two months, I'm going to master the class like I am with so many other things in my life right now.

Me. Annabel Conway. Who would have thought? Me, that's who.

Chapter Twenty-Six

140.2

The bell rings and I slam my locker closed. Em's standing next to me and we're ready to go to our first class. It feels so strange being back at school. Especially since I've only been here for fifteen minutes and I'm pretty sure everyone in the whole school has stared at me and half of them have come up to talk to me. Told me how good I look, acted like we've been best friends for years. I'm nice, tell them thank you and promptly hide behind Em.

Because even though this is what I thought I wanted over three months ago, it's not.

Okay, let me rephrase that: it is. I wanted to lose weight. Wanted to be healthier. Wanted to prove to myself that I could do it, but back then I also wanted to prove a point to the Billy's of my school. I wanted the boys to drool and the girls to be jealous. Maybe that makes—or made— me a shallow person. Or maybe it just made me someone who wanted to shine for once, which I don't consider a bad thing. I'm not sure which it is. What I do know is, standing here, twenty five pounds lighter, I'm happy. I feel good about myself, but it's not because all these people are staring at me. It's not because I've had people tell me how good I look or because suddenly it's okay to be my friend.

It's not even because I've lost weight. Being overweight doesn't make a person someone to be ashamed of, just like being skinny doesn't make you someone to be proud of. No. What matters is on the inside. How you feel about yourself and how you treat others. I've accomplished something and found *my* self-worth. I couldn't give a crap about Billy Mason anymore. I care about Annabel Conway. I care about my friends—my true friends. Em, Sandra and April. We've been texting back and forth and even met up at the mall once. Em likes them, and they like her too. And it's hard…so hard not to ask them about Tegan. To tell them I don't want to hear it when they talk to me about him, but I do it. Even though I still love him, I find a way not to go there. I'm not ready yet.

"Billy Mason, twelve o'clock," Em whispers in my ear.

I look over to see Billy, Patrick and the rest of their crew walking down the hall. The sea of students part, letting the shark wade through the water until he stands in front of me.

"Wow…Lookin' pretty hot, Conway."

Okay, is it me or is he the biggest idiot alive? Lookin' hot, Conway? I'm not sure that's cool in any universe. Especially one where he's given me hell for years and picked a fight with my boyfriend. "You must have worked on that one all night. I have to say, your line could use a little more work though."

I start to walk away, but Billy's hand on my arm stops me. "Listen, Conway." He steps closer to me and lowers his voice. "Can we go somewhere to talk?"

Instead of holding my thoughts in, I find myself saying them. "Are you for real? No. Actually, *hell* no."

"Aw, come on. Is this because of your boyfriend? Listen, I didn't mean to kick his ass, but he started it."

My heart jumps at the word boyfriend when it's attached to Tegan. "It has nothing to do with Tegan and all to do with the fact that you're an ass. That just because I've lost twenty-five pounds you automatically decide to try being friends with me. What? Because I fit in now?"

"No, it's because you're hot now." Billy laughs and all his friends fall into step, laughing with him. How does that make him funny?

"And you're a jerk. How shallow do you think I am? After everything you've done to me, you think just because you decide to show me attention now I'm going to fall all over you?"

"I—"

"No. I didn't say you could talk yet. You made me feel like crap. I didn't fit into your little definition of perfect and you never let me forget it. I can assure you, there is nothing. Nothing that would ever make you worth the air you breathe."

"She told you," Em says from beside me.

Just like the end of school last year, we're surrounded by people. This one will end differently. All of us are going to be late for class, but obviously no one cares. Without another word, I hook my arm through Em's and we walk, not run, away with our heads held high, Billy gaping at us as we go.

Chapter Twenty-Seven

UNDECLARED

I take a sip of coffee, looking for a seat in the busy coffee shop when I hear her. "Annabel? Oh, sweetie. How have you been? We've missed you so much!" Dana's arms wrap around me, squeezing me so tightly I can hardly breathe. It's such a Mom hug, so loving, so sacred that I can't help but squeeze her just as hard.

"I've missed you too." So much. Almost as much as I miss Tegan. When she lets go, I want to pull her back in again. "Hey, Tim." I lean down and give him a hug.

"Hey! It's really good to see you. Wanna come over and put my brother out of his miser—ouch, Mom! I wasn't going to say anything. Just that Tegan's driving me craz—okay, I'll stop!" he says when she smacks his arm again.

My senses go on high alert at the mention of Tegan. What was Tim going to say? I try to push those questions out of my head, but it doesn't work. The best I can do is cover them with a blanket for now. "What are you guys doing here?" Can you say stupid question? Dana holds up her coffee cup.

"I needed some caffeine."

"Yeah, me too!" It's then I realize Em's with me and I haven't introduced them. "Dana and Tim, this is my best friend, Emily. Em this is Tegan's mom and brother."

"Hi, Emily. It's wonderful to meet you." Dana shakes her hand and Tim tells her hi. Em shyly tells them hi back.

"Look at you!" Dana pulls me in for another hug. "You're a hottie. You've always been gorgeous, but watch out world!"

Her words make me giggle. "I don't know about hottie, but thanks."

"I'm serious. You look fantastic. You should be very proud of yourself. I know Tegan will be proud of you, too."

Will be. She says that like we'll see each other again. I mean, maybe we will, but maybe we won't. It's not a for sure. We're broken up. Over. The only time I've heard from him since the break-up was the happy birthday text. Still, I know the truth. "Yeah, I think he would be." A pang of sadness hits me. I'd like to share it with him. Even though we're not together, I wish I could show him I did it all on my own. That he was right, I didn't need him.

"Annabel, I have my first game tonight." Tim wheels closer to me. "It's a real game too. Not just practice. You should come and check out all my new skills."

"I…" Would love nothing more than to go to his game. To watch him play, talk to Dana. I miss them so much. Bubbles of excitement fizz inside me, but then I realize it's *Tim's* first game. Nothing would keep Tegan away from that. I can't just show up there, the ex-girlfriend budging in on his family time. "I'd love to, but I don't know if it's a good idea."

Dana grabs my hand. "Annabel, we'd love to have you. I'm sure *all* of us would love to have you."

Biting my lip, I look down at our joined hands. I'm not so sure of that. If that was the case, then why wouldn't he have called me in all this time? Sure we broke up, but we could have been friends. All of a sudden, I'm *mad* at him. Why can't we be friends? Why did he completely cut me off? It's not as if we broke up on bad terms—I guess any break up is bad, but it's not like we were angry. Unless there's something on his side I don't know about.

"Come on, Annabel. Please?" Tim gives me eyes. I recognize them, big, pleading and dark brown. Some girl is going to be in trouble one of these days because he knows how to work them just as well as his brother does.

His brother who isn't going to keep me from enjoying Tim's game. I shouldn't be scared to see him. If he's angry, oh well. There are a few things I'd like to say to him anyway. "You know what? I'd love to come and see your game tonight. What time should I be there?"

***

Wow, this idea felt much better this afternoon than it does now. My heart is thudding as hard as the basketball does when it hits the pavement. But I'm here. That's all that matters. If I see him, I do, if I don't, I don't. I wave at Tim while I walk around the court. When I get to the bleachers, I spot Dana sitting in the bottom row. Alone.

He didn't come. At first, I'm hurt and then—well, then I'm pissed. How can he miss his brother's game just because I'm here? The Tegan I know wouldn't do this. "Hi." I sit down next to her. "He's not here." We both know who he is.

"No he's not. I'm not sure why. He's supposed to be."

She may not be sure, but I am. He's not here because he knows I am. A cry threatens to crawl up my throat, but I block it out. "I should go…"

Dana shakes her head. "Why?"

I feel bad that she has to do this. That she has to lie to me so she doesn't hurt my feelings. That one son has to miss her other son's game because I'm here. "I just think it's better." I did what I came to do. I can be proud of that. I risked seeing him, but I'm not going to come between him and his family.

"Sweetie," she grabs my hand. "I don't know what happen with you guys, but I have a few good guesses. This doesn't excuse him, but his heart was in the right place. And he's hurting too."

She lets go of my hand when her cell phone rings. "Hold on a second. Let me get this, but you don't go anywhere, young lady." She winks at me, then walks away to talk on her phone. I watch her pace back and forth, just out of earshot, talking animatedly to whoever is on the phone. Is it Tegan? Do I care? I shouldn't, but I do. I know I don't need him, but I do still love him and somewhere inside me there's the girl who couldn't wait to see him today.

Before I can think about it much longer, Dana is back. "You're right. I think you should go, sweetie."

My chest hurts. My heart breaks. It sucks. It's painful and I hate it, but that's life, right? We all lose people and all you can do is move on, no matter how much you wish you didn't have to. "Will we still see each other?" I ask, hugging her.

"We will see a lot of each other. You're stuck with me now, kiddo. I always wanted a daughter."

A few tears leak out of my eyes and I hug her tighter. Before I lose it completely, I stand up. "I'll see you soon then."

"You're going home, right?"

I nod, wondering why she's asking. After another wave to Tim—one where I can tell he's confused as to where I'm going—I leave the building, get in my car and drive home.

***

The second I pull onto my street, I see it. See *him,* leaning against his old, beat-up car like he's done so many other times. Only now he's on my street. He's at my house. My heart accelerates along with my car. *Calm down, Annabel. You don't know why he's here.* And I'm not happy with him. In fact—I slam my car into park and get out.

314

"What do you think you're doing missing your brother's game?! He was so excited and you know he wants you there. I know you want to be there! How could you not go just because you knew I would be there?" It's only the beginning of what I want to say to him.

Tegan pretends to duck for cover. "You're not going to hit me again, are you?"

I bite my tongue to keep from laughing. Ugh. I missed him. I missed him way too much. "This isn't the time to joke, *Gym Boy.*"

"I know." He looks totally serious. The smile gone, his body tense as he no longer leans against his car, but stands up straight. Then, he hands me a piece of paper.

"I…"

"Just open it."

"I…"

"Please?"

"Only because you asked nicely."

He doesn't smile when he says, "Thank you."

Slowly, I unfold the paper. It's a college form. His college form, where he can declare his major. The box that's checked reads, "undeclared".

My hands start to shake. I'm not sure what to think. "You're not going to be a physical therapist?"

He shrugs. "Maybe. Maybe not. I'm not sure. I figure I don't have to decide right now. I can take classes, take some time, to see what I want to do. It's a big decision, you know."

Joy and hope spread through my body, warming me. He deserves to be happy.

"This past six weeks have killed me, Annabel Lee. I missed you so much, but I was so pissed. First at you because I loved you so much, but I couldn't have you. Then at me because I realized—"

"You couldn't have me?" Six weeks of pain, questions, anger explode from me. Things I should have said that last day, but was too scared. "You had me, Tegan and you threw me away! And why? You know I love your family. I would have understood anything you needed to do with them."

"I know." He stands there, waiting for whatever I throw at him.

"You *hurt* me, Tegan. More than anyone in my life because I *trusted* you more than anyone else." I don't know where it comes from, but I poke his chest with my finger. "And you threw that away. The first time something bad happened, you left me, just like—"

"My dad." His eyes fall closed and he lets out a deep breath, before opening them again. "I did exactly what my dad did. When I didn't know how to handle something, I ran."

Oh. I hadn't expected him to see it. "I thought I had to be everything for them. That letting myself have something for *me* meant I wasn't giving them what they deserved."

My hands are wiging out so much, I don't know what to do with them, so I shove them in my pockets. "You're only human, Tegan. You're nineteen years-old! It's okay to love them, but you can't dedicate your life to them."

"You're right...I can't and they don't need me to anyway. I don't know why I didn't see it, but I see it now."

Thump, thump, thump, thump, thump. I try to focus on slowing my heart, but I can only focus on him.

"I... I went and saw my dad. Told him how I felt about him. I talked to Mom and she told me how much of a conceited, big head I am. Timmy called me a dumbass and Mom didn't even tell him to watch his mouth. I needed to get over myself. Stop feeling sorry for me, for them. Stop thinking I could handle everything, because I couldn't and I don't want to. Why was it my job to save them? Be there for them? Yeah. Save them? No. They're not even the ones who needed it. It was me."

317

I can't explain how hard it is not to reach out and grab him now. Not to wrap my arms around him. Not to taste him. Not to soak up all his ocean and boy scent. But I can't. Not yet. "No one can save anyone else, Tegan. I've learned that. We all have to save ourselves."

"I know, baby. I know. Everything I've done the past few weeks has been the right thing, but it still didn't feel right. It didn't feel good. And then Timmy had his game tonight and I knew what was missing. *You.* I want to hold your hand while I watch him. See your face light up while *you* watch him. If you're interested, we can go to his game… Maybe talk some more after? We're going to be late. I called my Mom a little while ago and told her I came here first. She said to give you another half hour. I swear that woman is psychic sometimes."

He didn't miss the game to avoid me.

He didn't even know I was there.

And he's the one who called Dana.

She's the one who sent me home.

I can't help it, I laugh.

"Talk about a buzz kill. You laughing at me was the second worst way I imagined this going." He gives me his half smile. The playful one, but his eyes are still unsure. They're pleading with me.

318

"I was at the game. I saw your mom and Tim at the coffee shop and they invited me. I thought you weren't there because you found out I was going. Then someone called— which I now know was you and your mom told me to go home."

"She played us. That sounds like her." He bites his lip. I've never seen him look like this before. "Or maybe she just wanted to give us the chance to talk in private. Are you up for it? Talking, I mean?"

"What about the game? That's important."

Tegan steps closer to me. Not too close, not enough to touch me, but enough so I smell him. I want to wrap myself in that scent. In him.

"It is, but you're important too. There will be other games."

The old me wouldn't have said this, but the new me can't hold it in. I sit on the curb and he goes down beside me. Even though my voice shakes. Even though my eyes are wet, I still open my mouth and say, "You broke me, Tegan."

He runs a hand through his hair, pushing it away from his face and I see his eyes are wet. Wet with unshed tears like mine.

But it wasn't all his fault, was it? "I thought you were perfect."

"I know. I'm so far from perfect it's not even funny."

"And you shouldn't be. It wasn't fair for me to see you that way. You'd said it so many times about my mom, Em, me. No one is perfect. We all screw up, but I wanted—no, I needed you to be perfect because I saw myself as such a mess." I clear my throat, hoping to stall, knowing my words are true, even though I didn't know it until right this second. "Even if you didn't break up with me then, somehow, we would have fallen apart."

Tegan turns on the curb to look at me. His eyes are red. There's none of his cockiness there. Nothing between us. "No, I love you. We broke up because I screwed up."

"No, we would have regardless, because I needed you. It shouldn't be like that. Love should be love. Want should be want. You can love someone with all your heart. They can *be* your heart, but you have to be able to stand on your own and I couldn't." These words hurt so much, but they're freeing too.

"You never needed me, you just thought you did."

There is my truth. I thought I needed him, but I didn't. The only person I need is myself. It took losing him to know how to stand on my own. Now—now I know that regardless of my weight or who my boyfriend is, my friends are, or how anyone else feels about me, I really do measure up. I know how to stand tall and the amazing part is, he does too. I was his crutch as well, I just didn't know it. "I know. Now, I know that I didn't need you."

Tegan smiles at me. The first real smile he's given me today. "I needed you too. I don't anymore, but...I want you." I shiver when his hand slides through my hair. "I missed this, how soft your hair is."

"I missed you too." My eyes are closed and I'm leaning into his hand.

When he speaks again, his voice is so soft, soft, but strong, firm in what he says. "You're so beautiful, Annabel Lee. Inside and out. I'm so proud of you."

"I'm proud of you too."

"Open your eyes, please." There's so much heartache in his voice, that I can't help but do what he asks.

"Maybe I don't deserve to ask you this, but I'm going to anyway. I want another chance. I want us to be together, with nothing in between us. No need, no pain, hurt, fear. I want us together because we want to be. Because we love each other. I'll never leave you again."

It takes me a couple minutes before I can find my voice. He loves me. He wants to get back together with me. And I want that. We both want that. Not need. There's a huge difference there. It's like the air between us is clean. It's always been pure, because we've always really loved each other, but now we're *ready* to be in love. Ready to be together. "I missed jogging with you. I missed talking to you. I missed your big head. I love you too and I want to be with you so much it hurts."

My words are cut off by his mouth. I still know his movements so well. Know when to give, know when he's going to take. I fall backward in the grass, Tegan leaning over me, tasting me deeply. Too soon, the kiss is over.

"I love you, Annabel Lee."

"I love you, Tegan Edgar Collins."

"Want go to back to my apartment? I bet my mom and brother are still gone—ouch. Good to see you still hit."

"Good to see you're still a pervert."

He stands, and pulls me to my feet. "Okay, so plan number two. We go finish the rest of Timmy's game, and then go get physical."

I smack his arm again.

"Ouch! I meant go for a jog! You know, for old time's sake. Who's the pervert now?"

I shake my head and grab his hand. "Come on. Let's go." It's not him setting the pace and me trying to catch up or vice versa. We walk away together, equal.

The End

Acknowledgement:

As always a big thanks to my hubby and children. I love you all so much. To my Trio of awesomeness: Jolene Perry, Wendy Higgins, and Kelley York. Anyone who pre-read Annabel and Tegan's story: Kate, Jen, Jenny, Kristy and I hope I'm not forgetting anyone else. A thanks to my awesome friend Steph Campbell just for being you. It's amazing how much easier everything is when you have the incredible people in your corner that I do.

Also, to any and all readers who have given any of my books a chance. That means the world to me.

Made in the USA
Charleston, SC
21 February 2013